A Ghostly Affair
By
Joshua Griffith

ISBN: 978-1-7350784-4-1

Contact Joshua Griffith on Facebook

Follow him on Twitter

Or on BookBub

Table of Contents

To Midnight, the best familiar a witch could ask for

Chapter One
Portland Oregon, circa 1892

Thunder rumbled in the night sky above as Daniel Powell ran through the thick forest in a panic. He was constantly looking over both his shoulders, fearful that he's being followed. The rain hadn't started yet from the thunderstorm that loomed overhead but with each flash of lightning, it created shadows everywhere. With each flash, his eyes darted frantically as his mind played tricks on him or at least he hoped it was only that. His heart was racing as he slid around a large ever-green tree to take cover, pressing his back against it.

Daniel peered timidly from behind the tree, watching for any signs of movement in the dense forest. He silently cursed himself as the winds picked up all around him.

Why did I go to her, of all people? I'm such a fool and now I'm as good as dead!

Behind a large stone, Daniel could barely make out the slight silhouette of a man, if you could call it a man. Its black eyes were staring directly at him, pulsating slightly. It made all the hairs on the back of his neck stand up as a cold chill traveled down his spine, making him believe that his soul was fleeing his body and yet, he was too terrified to move.

The shadowy thing lifted what had to be a tendril for an arm toward Daniel and then it spoke, its voice was hoarse and raspy, but with each word that the dark entity uttered, it filled Daniel with dread.

"Why do you flee from me, Daniel? I'm only here to help in your time of need."

Daniel pulled out a wooden cross from his trouser pocket with a shaky hand. He mustered up what little courage he had to put it up in front of himself and the shadowy thing as a shield and shouted, "Back, you devil! You're no friend of mine nor do you wish to help me!"

The shadowy figure pouted, *"Daniel, I'm hurt by your actions. I truly am here for you. Why must you insist otherwise?"*

Daniel stammered, "Be…because you murdered that woman! You're evil so leave me be or -"

"*Or you will what, Daniel?*" Daniel couldn't see its actual face but could feel it smirking, "*Do tell me because now I'm intrigued.*"

"In the name of the Father, the Son, and the Holy Ghost, I compel you to leave me! In the name of the Father, the Son, and the Holy Ghost, I compel you to leave me! In the name of the Father, the Son, and the Holy Ghost, I compel you to leave me! I rebuke you, devil!"

The shadowy figure wavered slightly as the rain began to fall. As it dissipated, it mockingly cried out to Daniel, "*Storm's coming so if I were you, I'd go check on that beautiful family of yours. I believe something terrible will happen to them if you're not with them tonight!*"

Daniel panicked as he pushed himself from the tree and rushed through the forest once more. *Is Sybil in danger? Was that- that thing right about my precious family or is it trying to scare me?* Daniel wished that he had never struck a deal with that witch! Daniel was desperate for anyone who could help him and his family.

His wife Sybil and his two youngest boys had contracted an illness that left them all yellow skinned, a lot of skin lesions, and too weak to move around. Daniel spent all his money bringing in physicians to check out his family in hopes that they had a cure for this debilitating disease. Unfortunately, each doctor had said the same thing to Daniel: Bed rest, take whatever tonic they offered up, and it was all in God's hands now.

Daniel grew more frustrated with all the professionals with each passing day and decided to seek help from those whom his own church would condemn and possibly him too for associating with, such as witches and shamans to name a few. Daniel hated seeing his family suffering in so much pain and agony and all the tonics given to him didn't help. *Damn my soul to Hell,* Daniel thought, *I'd rather protect my family and save them from this terrible illness than care what others think of me and my actions!*

The rains came down hard and fast, like someone had fired a round of buckshot into the dark clouds above and now it was unable to hold back its contents. Daniel found that the ground was now more treacherous and slicker from the heavy downpour. The fall leaves and loose soil caused him to slip and slide multiple times, but he didn't want to slow his pace.

My God, please let my family be safe and okay!

Daniel's body shook as his clothes became waterlogged, clinging to his body. He was constantly having to swipe his long brown hair from his face and didn't notice the large embankment ahead of him. He fell head over heels into a creek that was usually calm and shallow. With heavy downpour, Daniel found it difficult to keep from getting swept away in the current.

He bobbed in the water until he was pushed into a large felled tree. He half stood up with his back against the downed tree to get his bearings when he heard the unmistakable voice of the shadowy thing.

"Hurry Daniel…Sybil along with Timothy and John need you home…You better move or else you will lose everything…"

Shit! How is that possible?

Daniel knew he spoke his words of his faith and it should've gotten rid of that thing, so how is it that it is still around here! Daniel's face paled even more as he recalled that it had used the names of his wife and two children.

How did it know their names? What kind of monster is this? *Was it really here to help me and my family or did it want to drag our souls to Hell?* That thought helped spur Daniel into action as he turned around and scrambled on top of the felled tree. It was slick in certain spots from where the moss patches grew, but Daniel knew that he had to cross the creek and fast before it swelled more and became impassable.

The felled tree didn't go all the way across the creek, but it was long enough that he could possibly jump to the other side. With grim determination, Daniel bolted as fast as he could, praying that he didn't hit a slick spot. As he was about to make his leap, a flash of lightning appeared somewhere in front of him, then came the booming sound as a thunder bolt struck a tree not far from him. It startled him so much that he leaped before he should have and ended up in the creek, twisting his right ankle.

Daniel howled in pain as he grasped at the injured ankle while the current swept him downstream. He bobbed in and out of the water, constantly having to spit it out. His eyes darted around, looking for a way out of the fast-churning water.

Is this to be my fate? Drowning as I try to save my family?

Daniel wasn't sure if this was God's way of punishing him for seeking out the help of a witch. The lightning bolt that startled him made him believe this, but why not just strike him down? Was drowning a more suitable punishment?

Daniel found himself rolling constantly with the current before he struck something hard and unmoving. Daniel grasped at whatever it was because he felt his body being pulled under it. Through bleary eyes, Daniel saw that it was a wooden raft used to fort across the creek whenever its water rose too high. It was used to safely get people on horseback or wagons with a lot of supplies needed to cross without losing their goods. The only thing keeping it from floating away down the creek was a long, heavy-duty rope that was tethered to a wooden post on the bank.

Daniel managed to hoist his body up onto the wooden raft as he tried to catch his breath. He spastically coughed up more water from his lungs. He looked up and saw that he wasn't too far from his cabin in the forest. Off in the clearing, there was the wagon trail that was several hundred yards from him that he used whenever he and his family went to town. This was all the encouragement that he needed, but as Daniel stood up, the pain from his twisted ankle came screaming back to the forefront that he nearly toppled back into the creek.

He managed to stand up as he gingerly put weight on his twisted right foot and hobbled over to the bank, thanking God that the raft was stationed on the right side of the creek. He snatched up a large tree branch and used it to help him move along the slick terrain.

I'm coming Sybil!

Daniel gritted his teeth as he hobbled towards the wagon trail, wondering if he would make it home to his family in time. Did that thing know something that he didn't? Was their sickness so bad that they may die tonight? Daniel shook his head as he muttered to himself, "If that were the case, then why was it wanting me home in the first place? It's not like I have a cure for them."

Daniel hobbled along the middle of the worn wagon trail as his mind started to fill with dreadful thoughts. Was there someone coming to harm his family? Did the shadowy thing see in the future or is it the one threatening his family? If it was, how could he stop it? Daniel wasn't sure what he needed to do to protect his family, but with a grim determination, he would find a way. He quickened his pace but no matter how fast he went, Daniel felt like he was moving at a slug's speed. As the forest engulfed him and the wagon trail, Daniel's paranoia crept back into his mind once more as every little sound made him flinch.

Daniel got the sense that someone or something was behind him but chose to move forward. *No sense in getting worked up over nothing,* he laughed inwardly but then he paused when he noticed something was touching him. Whatever it was, it sent chills up and down his spine. Daniel spun around and what he saw made him turn pale with fear.

The witch, the one he went to for help and the one the shadowy thing killed earlier tonight was standing in front of him. Daniel stumbled backwards and fell down as his feet got tangled up by the large stick in his hand.

This isn't real, this isn't happening!

Daniel fearfully gazed at the witch and noticed that he could see through her, like a hazy window. She seemed sad but also had a determined look in her eyes as she spoke with an ethereal voice, "Daniel...*where are you off to in such a hurry?*"

"B-back to my family, I-I'm needed there."

"I must insist that you stay away from there…"

Daniel looked at the ghost in bewilderment and wondered if she knew more about what was happening with his family. Why would the shadowy thing want him with his family? Why did the ghost of the witch tell him to stay away? He narrowed his eyes as he growled, "Witch! You give me one good reason as to why I shouldn't go be with my family. Your little pet has told me that they need me so I'm going to go to them!"

"Did it say why you had to go home?"

"Only that they were all in danger and that I should be there or I will lose everything!" Daniel spat out as he rose to his feet gingerly, using his stick to keep upright. He turned his back on the ghost and moved at a brisk pace. His ankle was screaming in pain, but as cold as it was, it was more tolerable to walk on.

"Did you stop and ask what the danger was or are you blindly heading into this fight with no knowledge?"

"No. It only said that I'm needed there now or I will lose everything! Did you not hear that the first time or do ghosts have memory issues?"

The ghost harrumphed as it glided next to Daniel. He glanced over at her and saw that she wasn't actually walking, but floating. He sneered at the dead witch as he spat, "Go away! I should have never sought you out in the first place and now you wish to haunt me?"

"I'm not haunting you!" The witch exasperated retorted, *"I'm trying to help you, which is why you came to me in the first place! I may be dead but that doesn't mean I can't help you save your family!"*

"You conjured that- that abomination and now my family is in danger!" Daniel scoffed, "How was that thing supposed to help you cure my family? Does it do your master's dirty work in exchange for our souls?"

"I have no master over me! How many times do I have to say that you're the one who believes in

the Devil, not I. Your faith has you believe in this, whereas mine is- was more nature-based and real!"

"If that's so, then why did it kill you?" Daniel asked as he grimaced while keeping up his steady jog, "If you ask me, you're not a very good witch."

"No one asked you and the reason it killed me was…it wanted what I had."

"And that was what? Certainly, it wasn't for your youth, you old hag!"

"I had power and it got greedy so when the opportunity presented itself, it killed me outright so I wouldn't banish it and it took my power. "

"If you have no power, how can you possibly stop it?"

The ghost bit her bottom lip, *"It will be more difficult but I can do it, which is what it fears, so now I'm here like this, to stop it."*

"Only fitting for the likes of you! Dabbling in things so dangerous and now it can roam the countryside, doing God knows what! Is this form to be your punishment for what you did? You created this problem, now go fix it!"

The ghost got in Daniel's face, making him pause mid stride, and fumed, "*And why was I "dabbling" in the first place? Oh, that's right, because you wanted my help! You came into my home, begging me to help save your sick family, all the while you cast disgusted gazes at my craft! That creature had aided me in the past and now it's free to do whatever it wishes because I lost my focus trying to help out the hypocrite that stands before me! Why didn't you just pray to your God for help? Why didn't you listen to the doctors and heed their advice?*"

Daniel stammered sadly, "I-I couldn't accept it! N-nothing worked and I grew tired of seeing my family writhing in pain and slowly withering away. Would you not go to the ends of the Earth to save the ones you love?"

"*I wouldn't have to since I'm a witch! Now that you screwed me over with your pious judgment of my craft, I say this with all the intent I have left in me. You WILL get EXACTLY what you deserve and the same goes for your family since you brought this upon them.*"

"A dead witch trying to hex me from beyond the grave? You're pathetic!" Daniel scoffed as he walked through the ghost. It sent shivers throughout his whole body but he didn't care.

I have to save my family!

The ghost floated beside Daniel, casting a baleful gaze, but he ignored her.

"Oh, it's not a hex my dear boy, but a promise. Soon, you will see it come to fruition and I hope that I'm around to see it when it occurs. Why do you hate me so much?"

"Because the Bible says that we should not suffer a witch, so -"

The ghost cackled loud and the sound of her laughter sent chills up his spine. She glared at Daniel with a smirk as she stated, *"Clinging to that book that you hold so near and dear to your heart? I say you're only paying lip service and you're not as devout as you claim to be. Don't try to deny it because I've seen proof of this."*

"What in God's name are you rambling on about? I've studied and read the good book and -"

"Have you now? If this is true, then why couldn't you banish 'my pet', as you put it?"

Daniel finally looked over at the ghost and was curious to know the answer to this so he asked, "Why didn't it work for me? I said the words and meant it, but -"

"But what, Daniel?" The ghost gave him a knowing look.

"I thought I'd gotten rid of it. I saw it disappear as it warned me, but then I heard its voice once more. So why in God's name didn't it work?"

"It's so simple, even a dead witch could see the problem and I did because I've been watching you this whole time."

"What did you observe?" Daniel asked with concern.

"You said the words with intent but because the faith you have in your religion is so shaky at this point in time, it failed you. If you're going to invoke your God to rebuke evil spirits, then you need to be completely unwavering in your beliefs. Otherwise, you're only speaking hollow words and that's why you failed miserably."

Daniel was prepared to deny this allegation, but in his heavy heart and troubled mind, he knew she spoke the truth. For months now, Daniel refused to go to church services and chose not to read any scriptures because it all paled in comparison to his dire situation with his family.

They were on death's doorstep and his pastor kept telling him to believe in God and leave it in His capable hands, but Daniel could see in the man's eyes that he knew that his wife and children were going to die. Hollow words and lip service? Yes, it was true and Daniel had been questioning his faith ever since then because it seemed like it was all talk and no action to him.

As the wagon path veered off the left, Daniel could see his cabin off in the distance. He could see the smoke billowing out of the chimney and the light from the fireplace lit up the windows with an orange haze that spoke of warmth on this cold, stormy night. Daniel smiled as he let out a sigh of relief as he noticed the shadow play in the windows.

My family!

Daniel threw down his stick and bolted towards his cabin. The ghost appeared in front of him, flying backwards with concern on her face.

"I can see my family! They're alive and that's all that matters to me, witch!"

"I know this, but they aren't alone."

"How can you know this when you've been glued to my side this whole time?"

"I can sense the one that killed me in there with them and...it's not doing them any good either."

Daniel slowed down as looked at the ghost. She seemed to be contemplating something when he asked, "What is it doing to them? Is it not healing them like it's supposed to do?"

"It killed me so all commands I gave it, it will ignore so now we must be cautious when we confront it."

Daniel frantically asked as tears streamed down his face, "Tell me what it's doing to them, please! If it's hurting them, how can we stop it?"

The ghost gave Daniel a sad look as she closed her eyes. Daniel couldn't stand idly by while she checked on his family, so he sprinted the best that he could while ignoring the pain in his ankle. Just as he got within twenty feet of his cabin, Daniel could see the shadowy thing inside and it appeared to be hovering by the fireplace. The ghost appeared before Daniel with a look of uncertainty. She instinctively reached out with her ethereal hand to touch Daniel on his shoulder and all it did was make him shiver more.

"*Sorry, old habits. Your family is still alive but only just. Whatever it's doing, it's killing them.*"

"NO!" Daniel blurted out as he ran for the front door. He pulled out his wooden cross and gave it a questioning glance. *Would this stop that thing? I couldn't get rid of it earlier so what would be different now?*

The witch's ghost floated beside him and whispered, "*I know you have doubts, but if you can believe in this, then your family might have a chance. I have a plan but I need you to go in first and draw its attention to you. I will do what I can to help you banish it."*

Daniel let out a gulp as he nodded. As he reached for the door handle, his anxiety was ratcheting up as he felt his heart racing like he was still running. Daniel clenched his wooden cross in hand so tightly that his knuckles became white.

Why did it want me here in the first place when all it wants to do is kill my family? Was this some sort of sick joke to make me run for dear life only to witness it killing my Sybil and the boys in front of me?

Daniel yanked the front door open and rushed inside and was greeted by the warmth of his fireplace and the shadowy thing. It seemed delighted that Daniel was here as it chirped up, *"Daniel, you made it just in time to watch me take care of your family! Do have a seat and enjoy the show as I bring them back from the brink of death!"*

"No, you're not! You're here to kill them all, I know it!"

The shadowy thing tsked, *"Daniel, you wound me with such mistrust. Who's been filling your head with such nonsense?"*

"You have! You've been saying that I had to hurry home or I will lose everything!" Daniel replied with a shaky voice.

"I wanted you here because your family won't live through the night. If you took your sweet time, they would have succumbed to the disease. Fear not, I've kept them alive, but I wasn't sure for how long. Now without further ado, I will heal them for you, as per our agreement."

Daniel looked at the shadowy thing wearily, having difficulty believing what he heard. *Was it really going to heal my family? Was the dead witch wrong in assuming it would do something worse?*

Daniel didn't know who to trust, but he did want his family healed and their sickness gone. He looked down at the floor and saw his wife Sybil lying prone while holding Timothy and John in her frail arms. They looked worse. His wife and children appeared more skeletal, their yellow skin drooping wherever it was visible and were covered in more lesions than before.

His heart was breaking seeing his loved ones in this condition, Daniel blurted out as tears streaked down his face, "Do it! Save my family please, I can't bear to see them suffer like this anymore!"

The shadowy thing made a hissing sound as it moved towards the prone bodies on the floor. As it hovered over his family, Daniel noticed that several black tentacles snake their way seamlessly into their bodies. Daniel wasn't sure why, but this didn't seem right to him and his fear and anxiety heightened more. The shadowy thing let out a low buzzing noise as it swayed back and forth, like it was in a hypnotic trance.

Is this how it heals people normally? Daniel still wasn't convinced that what it was doing was good. *Am I damning our souls for the selfish choices I've made on their behalf?* Daniel felt nauseated by this thought and wondered if there was a way that he could stop all this from happening. *They will never look at me the same way after this night,* Daniel thought, *especially if they knew how I cured them of their sickness.* He was happy that this thing may save their lives, but at what cost? The witch paid a terrible price in summoning this creature and Daniel wasn't convinced that it didn't have ulterior motives.

One by one, Daniel could see the skin lesions disappearing completely and slowly their skin went from a jaundice yellow to a vibrant pink hue. Daniel knew his family was looking better with each passing second, but for some reason he felt more anxiety and fear than anything.

This should be a joyous occasion so why am I so damn scared?

"Not much longer now, Daniel. Soon you will be reunited with your family once more…"

Even with its reassurance, Daniel wasn't convinced. *Why do I feel so uneasy about this?* Something kept nagging at him, like he was forgetting something or just missed…*Wait a minute, did it say that I will be reunited with my family? What did it mean by that? We are here now so how can we be reunited, unless it meant that they would be up and moving about shortly?*

Daniel paced nervously back and forth with his hands clasped behind his back, clenching his wooden cross tightly. He watched on as his family looked more alive, their skin and muscles sliding back into a normal, healthy position. They no longer looked emaciated or skeletal as they each moved around slowly.

Daniel jumped when he felt the cold, icy touch of the witch beside him. She put a finger up to her lips as she pulled out a dagger that had what looked like strange etching in the blade. She moved past Daniel just as his wife and children seamlessly stood up. Sybil still had her loving arms wrapped around her boy's bodies protectively, but none of them had yet to open their eyes.

"Sybil? Timothy? John? Are you well?" Daniel cried out with a shaky voice.

"They will be soon enough. You can't expect them to be running out here after what their bodies have been through these past few months."

Daniel walked towards his family, but the shadow thing gave him a stern warning, *"That's close enough. Any closer and you will* undo what I've done for them. You don't want to see what will happen to them if you disobey me."

As Daniel backed away, the shadowy thing hissed as it looked around the cabin and grew more agitated.

"What's wrong?" Daniel asked with concern, "Am I too close still -"

"*No, now be silent!*" the shadowy thing snapped, "*We aren't alone at the moment and I'm trying to ferret it out of hiding! Come out and show yourself, if you dare!*"

The ghost of the witch appeared behind the shadowy thing and stabbed it with her dagger. It howled in pain as the ghost twisted the dagger. The shadowy thing managed to grab a hold on the ghost and flung her in front of it. She hovered next to Daniel and said with malice in her ethereal voice, "*Like I told you Daniel, it's here to kill them all and won't help you!*"

"*Ah, so I'm going to be troubled with the witch once more, is it? I should've known you were the one filling his head with THAT nonsense!*"

The ghost smirked, *"If it's nonsense, then let go of his family. Prove to him that they are alive and well."*

"If I do that, then they will perish. You don't want that to happen now do you, Daniel?"

"Don't listen to it!" The ghost spat, *"It's manipulating you into thinking that your family is better."*

"Are you sure of this? What makes you believe otherwise?"

"When you are dead like I am, you can tell a lot about people and your family is dead and gone from this world."

"What!" Daniel cried out in a panic, "Do something, witch!"

"Gladly!" the ghost purred as she moved as fast as lightning at the shadowy thing, but then a strange light appeared between him and it. It chuckled manically as the ghost screamed out in anger, then the light and the witch ghost was gone.

Daniel stood there, dumbfounded and didn't know what to do. He glared at the shadowy thing as it still chuckled, so he lifted his wooden cross in front of him and shouted, "What have you done to her and my family? Answer me, monster!"

The shadowy thing replied smugly, "*I moved the witch on so she wouldn't try to kill me. Is that such a terrible thing? To rid the world of a ghost, a witch's ghost, I might add? You should be happy because I knew you despised her kind anyway.*"

"Is- is my family alive or was she lying?"

"*Time to find out for yourself...*" The shadowy thing pulled its tendrils from their bodies and they all collapsed down on the floor. Their bodies went back to looking sickly and emaciated once more as the shadowy thing cackled, "*It appears the witch was not lying and yes I did kill them. It was what you asked for after all.*"

"No, I didn't, I wanted them healed! I-"

"*No, your exact words were that you wanted them healed and to suffer no more. I healed their bodies, as you witnessed, but to suffer no more, they had to die. You got exactly what you asked for and with their deaths, they fed me so now I'm stronger and for that, I thank you, Daniel."*

Daniel put his hand up that held his wooden cross and was ready to attempt another rebuke, but the shadowy thing merrily laughed as one of its tendrils shot out and yanked it from his hand. It flung it into the fireplace as it got inches from Daniel's face and said coldly, *"It will take more than that little trinket of your religion to get rid of me now, boy! I grow tired of your antics. You chose to work with the dead witch and now want to fight me? I believe it's time to show you who's really in charge here tonight."*

Daniel looked down as he saw more tendrils fly into his chest. He screamed in agony as he felt them squeezing on his heart like a constrictor.

The shadowy thing laughed once more as Daniel collapsed on the floor and announced, *"Unlike your family, I will leave you here to wallow in misery and suffering, knowing that they all died because of you, Daniel. Because of your actions against me, I feel you deserve this and that's why I won't move you on, like I did with the witch!"*

Chapter Two
Portland Oregon, Present day

Brianna was busy texting on her phone as Jess drove along the dirt road leading them to their new home. Jess's parents had insisted that they buy this one since it was so cheap because most of the housing in the Portland area was skyrocketing at a ridiculous rate. Even apartment rentals were soaring out of control, so along with Brianna's parents chipping in what little money they had, they had to buy a place before things got worse.

"Why does this place have to be out in the fucking boonies?" Jess grumbled.

"Hey, it's not in the boonies. We're still in Portland" Brianna replied, trying to placate him.

"Since when does Portland have dirt roads to nowhere?"

Brianna rolled her eyes as she thought that Jess was in one of his moods again. Never happy about anything unless it's a video game or the latest piece of technology. She was relieved when she got the call from her mom that they found a place and that it seemed like the kind of home Brianna would love because of its location. As they drove down the dirt road, Brianna set her cell phone down on her lap and looked out the window, watching the trees pass. It felt tranquil and quiet, which caused Brianna to let out a soft sigh.

"This road is going to be hell on our car! Why couldn't they find a house that had a paved street?" Jess whined.

"It was either this place or keep moving from motel to motel because *someone* chose to take *our* rent money and blow it on a new computer!" Brianna snapped.

"That computer didn't cost that much for what it has in it. Besides -"

"You're right, I forgot to add in the new phone, as well as the three new Xbox games you just had to have. Rent money may not mean much to you, but a roof over my head does! I swear, I'm not sure why I'm still with you."

Jess slammed on the brakes and brought the car to a halt. He sat quietly for a moment, gripping the steering wheel tightly as the muscles in his jaw twitched. Brianna turned and watched Jess intently, waiting for his next tirade or excuse. He finally looked over at Brianna and said coldly, "You can get out and walk from here, you know. I'm sick of you treating me like a child all the time."

"Maybe if you behaved like an adult, we wouldn't be finding ourselves in these financial messes. This is a gift that we can't squander away like all the other places we've lived at before. How would you explain to our parents why I'm walking instead of in this car?"

"I'll tell them you're in one of your moods and went on one of your *walks*." Jess snarled.

"Yeah, your mother might buy that line of shit you're pedaling, but everyone else will know that we were fighting. Do you really want to piss on this happy day? If you do, that will be a slap in everyone's faces because they didn't have to do this for us."

Jess glared at Brianna for what seemed like an eternity to her before he put his foot on the gas pedal, focusing on the road ahead. Brianna looked down at her hands, no longer interested in playing on her phone. She didn't enjoy fighting with Jess, but lately that's all they seemed to do and it affected her more than she would let on to anyone around her. Brianna's health had multiple ailments, the biggest one was Fibromyalgia, and lately it's been taking a nose dive with all the stress and the constant moving from place to place. She wanted to contribute more to their financial situation because being on a fixed income didn't go so far, so she had taken on-line classes to be a freelance website designer.

So far, that has been their saving grace lately. Jess had difficulty keeping a steady income coming in because he was constantly getting fired for calling in sick too much. Brianna worried that one day they would be out on the streets. With too many close calls, it nearly came true, the witch lamented as she quietly sighed. As they drove over a concrete low-water bridge that was built over a large creek, Jess decided to comment, "They can build this, but not pave the road? Yes, this *will* be a great place to live."

Brianna ignored his snide remark and thought this would be a great place to come visit, if it wasn't too far from their new home. She could spend hours here by the creek, listening to the free-flowing waters, using it as an escape from being cooped up in the house all day! There was a small meadow between the creek and the rest of the surrounding forest. It appeared to be teeming with life as she watched several rabbits scurry into the underbrush, causing eight little sparrows to take flight.

She smiled as they drove into a naturally made dark corridor created by the old trees along the dirt path. It was feeling like home already and she hadn't seen the place yet. Jess was still sulking as they pulled into the driveway, where they were greeted by both of their parents. As Jess parked the car, the witch smiled as she muttered to him, "Wipe that attitude off or you will get an earful on multiple fronts."

"I will try, but this place looks like a dump." Jess retorted as he got out.

Brianna rolled her eyes as she climbed out of the car and was immediately greeted by her mother Anna. She hugged her daughter gently while casting a glare at Jess, who was walking over to his parents meekly.

"Are you okay, sweetheart?" Anna asked.

"Yeah, I am, mother," the witch replied innocently, "Why do you ask?"

"Because I can tell that you're not, don't try to deny it," Anna firmly said with a gruff voice that spoke of many packs of cigarettes she used to smoke, "You two are fighting again, aren't you?"

Brianna shrugged her shoulders, "Nothing new these days. It's good to see you though, mom."

"Nice deflection," Anna harrumphed as she looked her daughter over, "Since you won't say it, then you might as well take a look at your new home."

The witch walked beside her mother towards the cabin where Jess was chatting with his mother Jane and father William, doing his best attempt to look happy. Lee, Brianna's dad, was walking around the cabin, inspecting the craftsmanship and looking for any flaws left by the renovations. He was smoking on his cob pipe, nodded while muttering under his breath to himself.

"Your father thinks we paid too much for this place, even though it was priced so low that someone would be a fool to pass on it." Anna commented.

"How much did this place cost?" the witch asked, then added, "Not that I'm ungrateful or trying to be rude, but now you have me curious."

"I know you're not, so don't fret. You know your father, ever the tightwad, no matter what. But at $82,000, it does make you wonder what's wrong with it since it was built back in the late 1800s."

Brianna nodded as she gazed upon her cabin with wonder and questions of her own. Was there termite damage? Black mold? Brianna dismissed these since it had been renovated and inspected to ensure it was up to code to be a livable space, but why so cheap?

Did a murder occur here that kept it from selling or was it so old that the realtors wanted to dump it on the first bid they received?

Speaking of realtors, Jackie Stephens stepped up beside Lee and was chatting him up. Probably trying to keep him happy so he won't withdraw his bid. The woman looked out of place next to the cabin in her gray power suit and silk blouse, but at least she was wearing calf high boots instead of her designer pumps. Jackie oozed of money and the witch could tell that she wanted to hop back into her shiny black Escalade and leave this property as far away in her rearview mirror as possible.

The first thing Brianna heard come out of Jess's mouth since arriving, "Does this place have internet and indoor plumbing? I don't want to live here if it doesn't have that."

"Not to worry, Jess. This -" Jane waved her hand as she crinkled her nose in disgust, "the cabin has been modernized and updated so quit your bitching and be glad it's standing at all!"

"Both Lee and I gave the place a once over with Jackie," William stated as he nodded at Brianna and Anna with a benevolent smile, "it's a great place to call home away from the busy streets of Portland, but not that far from it either."

"I don't know if this place is worth calling it a *home*, but since you two are in a pickle, it will have to do for now." Jane strolled away towards her Cadillac, shaking her head in disgust. She looked over her shoulder and commanded, "William, I want to go now. This place stinks to high heaven and I want to be home before dark."

William walked over and hugged Brianna and gave her a peck on her cheek before heading towards his Cadillac. Anna watched him go and said under her breath, "That woman wouldn't know a good deal if it came up and bit her on the ass!" and then she bellowed out, "Lee! Leave the woman alone! The kids need a home so knock it off!"

Lee looked at Anna with his mouth open, but with a glare from her, he replied, "Yes dear."

Brianna and her mother strolled their way up to the newly added porch where Jess was leaning against the cabin, still giving their new prospective home a disgusted look. Jackie joined them and beamed a fake smile as she announced, "It's great to finally see the happy couple that will be residing in this cozy starter home! Are you ready to see the rest of it?"

Jess muttered sarcastically under his breath, "Yes, I'm dying to see the rest of this jewel."

Brianna smacked Jess in the stomach as Jackie unlocked the front door. As she pushed the door open, the realtor walked in cautiously. She looked around for a moment before turning around, donning her fake smile once more, announcing, "It may not look like much but it has two bedrooms and a full bath. The cabin has been remodeled and updated so it does have electricity and brand-new appliances. The best feature of this cabin, besides its old rustic feel," Jackie pointed, "is that hand crafted fireplace. Feel free to look around your new home!"

"When was this place built?" Lee asked as he checked the flooring with his foot.

"It was built back in 1890's. It was vacant for a long period of time before it changed hands over the years. During those times, the cabin has been restored and renovated while preserving its historical value."

"How long has it been unoccupied?" Brianna asked as walked over to the fireplace.

"Since it was first built, it was occupied for five years but after that, roughly a century before a property investor snatched it up in 1995. He was the one who made this place look immaculate, as you see it now."

Jess snorted while everyone glared at him as Jackie added, "Mind you, a hundred years of sitting unattended and unoccupied requires a lot of work and he has poured a considerable amount of money in this restoration project."

"He did a wonderful job on it. You say this was done back in 1995?" Anna asked.

"Yes, it took him nearly two years but since then, he's been making repairs and the upkeep has been getting too much. So, he decided to sell it, instead of renting it out any more."

Brianna let her hand caress the smooth rocks along the fireplace and got a sense of pride. To do this by hand back in those days would have been a great achievement and worth the effort because this would've been the only warmth for the whole family. She wondered what the family was like that built this beautiful cabin and why they would abandon it after five years. Times would have been difficult back then and there were more dangers from outlaws, the wildlife, and the hardships of the land, but Brianna wasn't convinced that these would force the former owners to leave.

Jess walked into one of the bedrooms, still looking gloomy from what Brianna could tell. *Is nothing good enough for him? Does a roof over our heads that we can call our own mean nothing to him?* She rolled her eyes as she turned around and saw Jackie was still rambling on about the other amenities that came with their purchase.

"The cabin comes with twenty acres of land which I took the liberty of having it surveyed so you will know where the boundary lines are located on this map and there are stakes out there to give your kids a physical marker too."

"Really?" Lee said with surprise. He looked over at Anna, "Did the ad mention this?"

"No, it didn't," Anna eyed Jackie with suspicion, "Why would the seller do that and for such a dirt-cheap price too?"

Jackie shrugged her shoulders slightly, "Your guess is as good as mine. I've tried to get him to reconsider this and at least raise his asking price, but he won't budge. He's dead set on getting rid of this property so his loss is their gain, I guess."

"You say he's had to constantly repair this cabin?" the witch asked as she stood next to her mom.

"Yes. Other than the usual wear and tear from the elements, it seemed that all who've rented this property have managed to trash and destroy it. You can understand how costly it can get renting a place out, having it trashed to the point that you have to spend four or five months to repair it properly. It went on like this for the last ten years and after the last tenant ran off, the seller gave up and decided it was time to fix this place up for sale."

"Guess he should've screened his applicants better," Jess laughed as he approached everyone.

"Just because a person passes a screening doesn't mean they won't trash the rental they're living in," Lee pointed out, "When me and Anna managed those apartment complexes, we had a strict and thorough screening and background checking system. We had some of the best renters and yet, there were ones that decided to destroy things before they left. It happens. You never know what an apartment will look like when someone vacates, you only hope for the best."

"It's like trusting the only apartment left to one of two applicants. One who's got a clean record and great rental track record or a fella that's had a rough go of it and all signs point to being untrusting so you pick the first fella and this person ends up demolishing the apartment to the point that it's unrecognizable.

So, I ask this: which category would you fall under, Jess?"

Jess shifted his feet uncomfortably under Anna's gaze, uncertain what to answer. He looked over to Brianna like she would be a lifeline in his time of need, but she cast him a knowing look as everyone waited for him to speak. The witch didn't feel sorry for him. Jess's attitude lately has been more condescending and mean-spirited sarcasm, but under her mother's scrutiny, none of that would fly.

Two things a person didn't do around Anna and that was cop an attitude and lie because the woman didn't take crap from no one and she could somehow tell if a person was lying. She never told Brianna how she did it and never elaborated, only saying that she "just knew somehow". The living room was silent. No one, not even Jackie made a sound because Anna's command of the room was that powerful. Lee made a slight motion with his hand, hoping Jess would say something.

"I…um…I'd say the second category, the one that didn't get the apartment." Jess answered as he put his hands in his pocket nervously, sweating as he hoped to give Anna the answer she wanted.

Anna crossed her arms over her chest and stared at Jess for a moment before giving a quick nod as she replied, "That's right and it's the reason we are here today. I want what's best for Brianna and at the moment, a stable home life is what she needs. All the crap you've been putting her through with the evictions and losing jobs left and right has taken a toll on our daughter. This is *your* one and only chance! We've all pitched in to get this place for the two of you, but if you can't hold down a job and be an adult, then maybe you should go live with your dad and entitled mom!" she pointed her finger at Jess, "No more bullshit, boy! If I have to grab you by your ears and drag you out of here, kicking and screaming, I will! Are we clear?"

Jess nodded frantically so Anna set her steely gaze on Jackie and asked, "How many renters did the seller have or do you know off hand?"

"He never said, but it sounded like they all followed the same pattern. Rent the cabin and after a few months, they would either pack their stuff up and go or leave everything behind without any notice. The seller is tired of this vicious financial cycle and is ready to be done with it forever. He will honor any repair work on the most recent repairs, but that's all he will do."

Brianna nodded but felt like there was more to it than this place being a money pit for the seller. She could tell Jackie was uncomfortable talking about her client and his money woes, but deep down, the witch felt that she knew more than she was letting on.

Brianna shrugged it off as she walked towards the open kitchen. The witch enjoyed cooking but with all the constant moving and her health tanking lately, she dreaded the kitchen, let alone doing the dishes. She nearly squealed when she spotted a brand-new flat surface stove top oven.

The last oven she had to cook with tended to run hotter than what the dials read and the metal coils on the stovetop were worse. There was a large island with a pristine, marble countertop that had a metal rack suspended above it where one could hang their pots and pans for extra storage space and above it was track lighting.

There was a two-door chrome refrigerator that matched the dishwasher, which looked like it was a step below being a commercial brand. *I can get used to this setup*, Brianna thought giddily. All the countertops were a dark gray marble and attached to the wall, just underneath the hanging cabinets, was a chrome microwave, so none of the countertop space was wasted. A small closet revealed a brand-new washer and dryer set. *Good gods*, the witch mentally squealed, *just this setup alone is enough to make a girl orgasm!*

Brianna couldn't resist opening all the drawers and cabinet doors because the need to see it all was overwhelming. Jess may not appreciate all this like she did, but if she's going to be doing all the cooking, she wanted to know how much space there was and work on organizing it.

The witch was brought out of her daze when she heard the word "death" coming out of Jackie's mouth. Brianna trotted back over to her parents and said, "What did she say about a death? Did someone die in this place?"

"The ones that built this cabin are the ones I was talking about with your parents. A husband and his wife and two children all died five years after this structure was built, all on the same night."

"Was it a murder or a murder/suicide combo?" Jess morbidly asked.

"Like I want to know that!" the witch scrunched her nose in disgust, "You've been watching too many police shows lately. What are you going to do, go all CSI: Oregon in our home?"

"Now that you mention it, that does sound like fun." Jess brightened up.

"I vote you leave the past where it's at. No sense in pestering things that happened a long time ago." Lee said as he looked around the cabin fearfully, which caught Brianna by surprise. Her father was the superstitious type and things having to do with spirits or the paranormal would cause him to behave like this, but today was the second time someone behaved like there was something or someone here. The witch looked at Jackie and noticed her eyes darting around.

"You think this place is haunted? Is that why you were so cautious when you entered the cabin?"

"Shhhh, Bri!" Lee whispered in a panic, "Don't say that, you might disturb them and that can be very unlucky for you!"

"Oh Lee, either throw some salt over your shoulder or go outside and smoke your pipe! Don't say you don't have any salt on you because I found a lot of those little packets in your pants pocket *AFTER* I washed them." Anna scolded as she pointed at the front door. Lee didn't hesitate to run for the door as he pulled out several packets of self-serve salt packets out of his pocket.

"Lee, this isn't your house and I won't have you salting their new home because you got freaked out."

"But- but Anna -"

"Just do it outside and you better empty your pockets next time you put your clothes in the hamper!"

"Yes dear!" Lee shouted as he ran outside, muttering a prayer under his breath.

Anna reached over and gently hugged Brianna with a sigh. She knew her mom was doing her best to make this visit to this place a memorable one for her and she appreciated it. Her dad had a habit of doing things to ruin occasions like this because he wanted to make things more about him. Lee tended to use his superstitions as his go-to weapon. The witch wouldn't have been bothered if her father threw salt over his shoulder, but that didn't mean she was going to steal her mother's thunder in stopping him. She had to live with the man, so why bother when it gave her mother some satisfaction?

"Jackie, is this place haunted or not?" Brianna asked as Jackie rubbed her hands together nervously.

"Oh, who cares, it's not like they can do much to us anyways." Jess said as he eyed one of the corners of the cabin, "As long as they don't interrupt me while I'm working -"

The witch cut him off, glaring at him, "You mean while you're playing WoW on the computer and claiming to be *"sick"* as you call in to miss more work?"

"You always make it sound way worse than it really is. I work hard so I deserve some 'me time' to play games." Jess whined to Brianna, but she said no more. She knew that it was his way of trying to start an argument, but now wasn't the time for his childish games. *He will never learn or grow up and yet again, I can see all the responsibilities for our new home will fall squarely on my shoulders*, the witch thought in disgust. Brianna looked at Jackie and said, "Well?"

"I can't say for certain if this cabin is haunted or not, but one of the former renters has spread it around town that it is. If what he said is true, it would explain why this cabin has been left in ruins after each renter leaves."

Curiosity piqued, Brianna inquired further, "So, what did he say?"

"Things being flung across the room, pictures getting tilted or yanked off the wall, doors opening and slamming, seeing the figure of a man but they could see right through it. It's creepy and it makes me think of that movie *Poltergeist*," Jackie shuttered.

"That's strange indeed, but I doubt it's an actual poltergeist."

"How can you be so certain of that?" Jackie asked with doubt in her voice.

"Yes Bri," Jess popped off with a smirk, "do educate us all? I'm sure your mom would love to hear your explanation."

Brianna's cheeks heated up. She looked over at her mom and saw she was giving her a quizzical gaze. Brianna took a deep breath and calmly explained, "The majority of poltergeist cases are due to repressed emotional feelings that tend to manifest through psychic means. If there were teenagers living in this cabin each time this place was rented, that would be a lot of psychic energy, but that's not likely."

"Are you saying that teenagers cause poltergeists?" Jackie asked as confusion caked her face.

"Yes, most of the time, especially during puberty, teenagers are more open and often it's their psychic abilities that they can be completely unaware of and it becomes a conduit for their emotions to spill out. Adults can cause it to happen if they don't properly deal with their pinned-up emotions. All those negative feelings that they've been hiding and have had no way of dealing with will come out. Like never resolving the feelings of losing someone close or never grieving over one's health when it decides to leave them all of a sudden…" Brianna trailed off, recalling how she felt when her healthy body betrayed her. She was an active, healthy girl that would go swimming, hiking in the mountains, or lifting weights with the boys in school just to show them that they weren't half as strong as she was.

One day, Brianna woke up and found herself in a hospital bed. She recalled getting out of the swimming pool at one of the many apartment complexes that her parents managed and getting ready to go out for a night of fun with her friends before blacking out. Brianna discovered, to her horror, that she had lost the use of her legs and was in considerable pain. The doctor that was caring for her told Brianna that she would never walk again. The witch stuck her chin out and told the doctor, "Watch me, asshole!", it may have taken her a good forty-five minutes to do it, but Brianna had managed to walk out of his office.

She had been diagnosed with Grave's disease, which is an immune system disorder where the body produces too much or not enough thyroid hormones. In Brianna's case, her thyroid was making too much of one type of that hormone, which was causing the issue. After going to see a specialist, they suggested giving her radiated iodine treatment, which killed her thyroid completely and meant Brianna would be on thyroid medicine for the rest of her life because without it, she would be in a wheelchair and extremely ill.

The treatment made her deathly sick, but Brianna managed to survive the lingering effects it had on her body several months afterwards. Brianna also had to deal with a severe form of Fibromyalgia, which causes her a great deal of pain and chronic fatigue throughout her entire body, making her more susceptible to other health issues ever since she was born. Brianna brooded and her anger increased exponentially during the rest of her high school years, unable to accept that her once healthy body had been snatched from her and now, she had to live in a pain-ridded, broken-down body.

Brianna, on her good days, can walk without hobbling or using a cane to steady her because she never received the proper physical therapy for her legs after she lost the use of them and now has muscle weakness in her thighs. Too much stress can put her into a fibro flare where every part of her body is sensitive and the pain is magnified.

With all the stress she had to deal with, the worse lately has been Jess. *How can I keep going through our relationship with it being so one-sided and his yearning to be a lazy slob that expects me to do everything for him since I'm on disability and can't work?* Anna looked at Brianna for a moment longer before hugging her and whispered, "I'm sure I understand that last bit, but the rest sounds so far-fetched to me. I'm not saying it's a load of bologna, I just don't understand things of that nature like you do."

"It…it did happen to me, mom. I had Uncle Frankie to help me get through the roughest part, but the rest I had to do on my own and accept it for what it was," Brianna shrugged her shoulders.

Anna gasped, "I knew you two were close, but I had no idea you were going through *THAT* horrible of a time. Mind you, I could tell being sick really got to you in so many ways. I felt helpless…I didn't know how to take care of my little girl."

"It's okay and what's done is done," Brianna replied stoically as she hugged her mom.

"So, if it wasn't a poltergeist, then what was it?" Jackie asked as she anxiously glanced around.

"Probably a pissy family of raccoons causing all the problems," Jess scrunched his nose in disgust, "This far in the woods, no telling what disgusting animals could have gotten in here and caused problems!"

"Yes," Brianna snapped back sarcastically, "because raccoons look human and you can see right through them. We live here now so get over yourself, Jess!"

"You have your opinion of this place and I have mine. Just because we live here doesn't mean I have to love it like you do, Bri. I'd rather be living downtown closer to work so I wouldn't have that far to commute."

Brianna stepped away from Anna and marched up to Jess and jabbed him his chest with her finger. She didn't care that he was a full foot taller than her, Brianna was 4' 10, because her mother taught her how to fight dirty and hold her own against bigger people.

As her grandmother would say, "Dynamite comes in small packages and so do we!" and Brianna took it to heart. She glared up at Jess as she growled, "We were living downtown a month ago and look what happened? You chose WoW over your work responsibilities and got your damn ass fired for it! I don't want to hear another pity party on this matter because you had what you wanted and you screwed the both of us! Do you think I enjoy wondering if we are going to have the electric shut off because you spent that money on a new game? If you don't wipe that condescending smirk off your face, I will do it for you!"

"See, Anna? This is what I have to put up with," Jess whined, "You should tell your daughter to get off my back!" he looked at Brianna and added, "I'm doing the best I can so get out of my face!"

"Bri doesn't need me to tell her what to do, Jess. It sounds like she knows exactly what's going on here so I'm not stepping into this mess." Anna shot back with a knowing look.

"I'm not in your face yet but I'm at the right height to drop you to your knees and then we will be face to face. So, knock off the attitude or I will drop you down to my altitude, in front of everyone."

Jess glared down at Brianna as his jaw muscles twitched. She knew he wouldn't do anything while her mom and dad were here, but once they were gone, Jess would go off on a tirade. Jess brushed by the witch forcefully and stormed out the front door.

Jackie looked at both Brianna and Anna before plastering her fake smile on again and said, "Well, I must say that was intense. Now, if you truly want to purchase this property, I have all the forms back at my office. You still want to buy it, don't you?"

"It's your choice, Bri," Anna put a hand on her daughter's shoulder, nodding towards the front door, "Do you want to live here or is there going to be a problem?"

Brianna looked around at the cabin, trying to find anything that could change her mind, but all it kept screaming was that this place was home and this is where she belongs. This place was calling to her as they drove along the dirt road that led to the cabin.

It's surrounded by a lush forest, a peaceful meadow as well as a freshwater creek. It felt like this spot was tailored-made for her and Brianna wasn't going to lose this place because Jess didn't approve of it. *It may not be a fancy, newly built house like he was wanting,* Brianna thought, *but it's our home so he should get over it or leave!*

"He won't be a problem, mom. I feel like I'm at home already."

Anna eyed her, "Are you sure about this?"

"We don't have much of a choice because of Jess's actions lately, but if I'm going to live anywhere, I want to live here. It feels right to me."

"Then your father and I will go get the moving truck and you two kids can start putting your furniture in this place."

Jackie motioned to the door with her fake smile beaming brightly because she was going to get rid of this property. As she walked with Anna, she paused to look over her shoulder and asked Brianna, "You're sure about this? Remember this place is supposedly *haunted*."

The witch shrugged her shoulders as she followed them out the door with a smirk, "If it's haunted, that's okay with me. I know a few tricks to clear out any unwanted spirits, if need be."

Chapter Three

Brianna carried several boxes in her arms as she came down the moving truck ramp, trying to get it unloaded as quickly as possible. Every move she made, each twist of her body and the steps she took up and down the ramp caused her pain to increase. The witch was grateful that her mother was helping her unload the truck.

Working in the apartment management business meant a lot of moving around, which Anna and Lee did frequently. Growing up, Brianna had to help her parents with each move because Lee had chronic pain in his left arm that made it difficult to move heavy objects, let alone hold on to things. The task of moving everything tended to fall on Brianna and her mother's shoulders and today was no different.

"I'm so glad to see you two moving in this cabin," Anna grunted as she carried down a large box that said *kitchen* on the side, "but really this would go quicker if we had more help."

"I know," Brianna gritted her teeth, trying to ignore the pain, "Maybe when Jess's parents get here, we can ask William to help."

"I think Jess should be out here helping more," Anna grumbled as they both walked into the cabin.

Brianna glanced over to her left and saw Jess setting up his bulky desk the way he wanted it. It may look neat and tidy now, but in a couple of days or less, it would be littered with junk food wrappers and his diet soda bottles. He was underneath it, setting up his computer tower as he grumbled, "I got all my stuff out of the truck already. The rest is Bri's crap."

"Ah, so that's the reason you're lounging in here?" Brianna snapped bitterly.

Jess sneered, "Hey it's not my fault you have so much junk. Maybe you should learn to get rid of some of *your* stuff and you wouldn't have to move so much."

Brianna dropped the boxes on the counter top with more force than she wanted.

She clenched her hands tightly; her anger began to boil over and warred with her pain.

Anna set her box by Brianna's boxes and said loudly with a smirk, "You have all your stuff in here already? Hmm, so where will he be sleeping, Bri?"

"Good question!" the witch said as her mood lightened up slightly, "He may have to sleep under his desk."

Jess crawled out from under his desk with trepidation and a weary look on his face. He brushed his pants off as he stood up and asked, "What are you two talking about?"

"Technically, that queen size bed in the back of the truck belongs to Brianna so since you say you have *everything* in here that you claim you need, then I guess that makes you shit out of luck in the bedding department."

Brianna leaned against the counter as she put her hands on her hips and glared, "I hope you brought your blanket and pillows in with that pile of boxes because you're not getting in *my* bed. Just know, if you didn't, I'm not looking for them."

"Fine, I will help but you need to help me with it." Jess muttered as he stomped out of the cabin.

The witch grinned as she pushed away from the counter and slowly walked over to the front door. Anna stepped up beside her and gruffly said, "You should take a break, dear. I don't want you to overdo yourself."

"I'm fine, mom. The faster we get all these boxes moved in, the sooner I can do that." Brianna replied, but nearly fell down as her knees buckled. She glared at her mom as she gave her a knowing look.

"Not a word, mom," she stated as she slowly straightened up and gingerly walked towards the front door. Brianna grunted under her breath, trying not to show her mom just how much pain she truly was in, knowing full well that she wasn't fooling her.

As she stepped outside, a light drizzle poured from the dark clouds above in the sky. Brianna closed her tear-laden eyes and took a deep breath. She loved nature, in all its many aspects, but the witch loved the rain the most.

It was both cleansing and soothing, which made her relax.

She opened her eyes and saw that her mom was in the moving truck, giving Jess an eyeful. As usual, he was nodding his head, but wasn't truly acknowledging what was being said to him. Brianna sighed, knowing this scene before her was the norm behind closed doors. She wished that she could make it on her own, but the paltry amount of income she got from disability meant that she had to stick with Jess.

The witch recently took up freelance website designing to help add to their income, but even with orders being scarce and with Jess having difficulty holding down jobs, it was a literal life saver, but not by much.

Brianna's biggest dream was to make enough contacts to land a lucrative paying job with some big corporation so she didn't have to rely on anyone else but herself. Unfortunately, that was what it seemed it would always be; a dream.

Being chronically ill with her many health issues forced her into this arrangement with Jess through their relationship. He never let her forget that with all her problems that no one would want her around, let alone be with her.

Just a week ago, he made a snide remark that it was nothing but a pipe dream to expect anyone to notice her amateurish attempts at website designing and to give up on the notion of getting noticed by anyone. Even recalling his hurtful word stung Brianna, despite getting inspiring, positive feedback from the clients she served. Jess's niggling words of doubt always had a way of making its way into her mind, no matter how many times she snuffed it out.

It wasn't always like this. Brianna had met Jess in Seattle at a small social gathering with a few of her coworkers when she worked at a temp agency. She found him to be a smart, fun guy and it didn't take long for the two of them to start dating. But that was almost ten years ago and as time went on, his demeanor and behavior subtly changed.

He came from an upper-class background and believed that he had that air about him, as well as the money. Brianna chalked up his snobby attitude to their new living arrangement to this. Jess tended to live beyond his means, which got them in hot water constantly over the past few years with not only the apartments, but the different utility companies.

It didn't help that his mother kept reinforcing this attitude, which caused strife between her and Brianna. Jane had the gall to try and control Brianna, as she would do with Jess, but the witch would have none of it. This friction affected her relationship with Jess, since he tended to follow his mother's lead, like an obedient child.

How did it get this bad, Brianna pondered?

Jess stood at the edge of the ramp, looking up at the drizzling weather with disdain and grumbled, "Great, it's raining again. Just what I needed while unloading all this crap."

Brianna walked past him and stated, "It's Oregon, what did you expect? It rains more here than anywhere else."

"I don't want all this stuff of *yours* to get all wet because knowing you, it will never get unpacked and the boxes will stink and get moldy."

The witch spun on her heels and got inches from her boyfriend, hands on her hip, and hissed, "Be thankful it isn't a damn downpour! It's raining barely enough to get your hair damp and it's not like you have far to unload. Also, all these boxes that haven't been unpacked, as you pointed out, remain that way because we are constantly having to move from place to place. How can I begin to set up a new home when the following week, we are moving once more?"

Jess sneered slightly as he stomped down the metal ramp with a couple of small boxes cradled in his arms. Anna stepped beside her daughter and gave her a side hug and rubbed her back, "Are you sure you want to do this? You know that you can come live with us. I can tell you're in pain and not just physically."

"I'm fine, mom," Brianna replied with frustration, "this is my bed and I have to lie in it. Besides, you guys already purchased this nice little cabin. No sense in it going to waste, right?"

Anna eyed her daughter in earnest, "If it means you being happy, then I'd let this place go back to the bank in a heartbeat. I know you and Jess are having a...rough patch lately, but that doesn't mean you shouldn't have an exit plan, which is me and your father."

Brianna stepped away from her mom and picked up a medium size box that had *clothes* written on the side and replied, "I'm grateful for the offer, but I'm an adult and I need to live my life the best I can. Trust me, there have been times that I've wanted to call you up and say 'come and get me!', but I know that would create a bigger financial burden on both you and dad. If I can get my website design portfolio in order and get more income coming in, then I could actually have some control over my life, financially."

Jess bounded into the truck, grinning as he sarcastically injected as he grabbed a decent size box, "You realize that's nothing more than a pipe dream. As if some large corporation would actually take a chance on an inept amateur like you? They tend to go with the best of the best, which leaves you out, *sweetheart*. You're nothing more than a dreamer."

He cackled and rushed out of the truck before Brianna could reply, leaving her stewing. She shook her head as she passed her mom on the way out of the truck.

Why did he have to behave like this?

The witch walked into the cabin, glaring at her boyfriend as she dropped her box on the floor. She wasn't sure why Jess enjoyed tearing her down. It's one thing to do it when they were alone but, in the presence of her parents, he was getting more brazen now.

Brianna found herself questioning her decision in staying with Jess and second-guessing her current career path. *Was he right? Am I just a dreamer? Am I simply diluting myself into thinking I have what it takes to be a successful website designer?* The witch mental asked herself.

Not wanting to argue, Brianna moved briskly back to the moving truck, passing her mom. She curtly shook her head in response to her mother's sympathetic gaze as tears threatened to flow from the corners of her eyes. She had a feeling that her mom would be giving Jess a chastising. If so, then more power to her. He needed it because Jess wasn't listening to her anymore.

Brianna sighed but took comfort in the fact that the back of the truck was ninety-five percent emptied. All that was left was the worn queen-size bed and its box spring, several boxes labeled *miscellaneous items*, Jess's ridiculously oversized computer chair, the folding dining table with four wooden chairs with mismatched cushions, and Midnight's blue standing cage.

Seeing his cage, Brianna can't help but touch it lovingly and think to herself: *Why did Jess stick my baby's home in the way in the back and not in the front?*

As if on cue, she heard her father's voice just beyond the thin metal wall of the box truck. He was questioning the intent of the bird as he asked, "Why do you keep doing that? You know it's not nice to nip at grandpa, don't you?"

"*Bad outside!*" Midnight screeched, "*Bad outside!*"

"I understand that, Midnight," Lee replies, "but do you have to keep trying to bite me? I'm -" he got interrupted as Midnight went into a barrage of high-pitched screaming. Brianna can hear her father attempting to speak above the screeching, but to no avail.

The witch rolled Midnight's cage down the ramp, meeting up with her father, who was carrying a small metal travel cage containing an agitated Nanday Conure. The bird was covered in several shades of green feathers that were ruffled up, his tail feathers had shades of black, blue, and green. His head feathers, along with his beak, was black as night

With pleading eyes, lips pursed, Lee asked, "Brianna, can you take this little guy and see what you can do with him?"

The witch nodded and took the handle on top of the cage while her father moved Midnight's regular cage inside the cabin.

"*Bad outside!*" Midnight screeched once more, "*Bad outside!*"

Brianna sympathetically gazed at the bird as she strolled into the cabin, right behind her father, soothing the Conure, "I know, Midnight, I know. The weather is icky today and you want to be inside where you feel safer, huh?"

"*Yes,*" Midnight stated with a pouty tone, "*Bad outside!*"

Brianna pushed past Jess, who was needlessly digging through one of the boxes he brought in, and set Midnight's little travel cage on the kitchen counter top. She leaned down by the tiny bars and whispered to the little bird, "It's okay, baby. We're inside now. Nothing can hurt you while you're inside."

Midnight listened intently as he slowly rocked his head back in a circular motion, calming down as she added, "Are you ready to see your *new* home?"

Midnight backed away on his perch and turned his little head, scanning the new environment. He cocked his head, giving Brianna a questioning expression, but then his eyes widened as he excitedly stated, "*Oh boy! New toy!*"

Lee stepped up beside Brianna and asked, "New toy? What did he mean by that?"

Confused, Brianna answered as she looked around, "I'm not sure exactly. I'm not seeing anything that would…"

Brianna trailed off as she watched the conure climb to the back of the travel cage. He stretched his neck as far as he could, pushing his sharp, pointy beak between the bars, attempting to touch the cabin wall. It dawned on her what got Midnight so thrilled, "The cabin, that's the new toy. This whole place is like one huge, wooden chew toy to him. This is going to be interesting."

Jess smirked as he pulled several computer cords from a box and snidely remarked, "Looks like someone will be staying locked up while we are living in this…*house*. Poor little thing."

"Hardly," Brianna answered as she opened the cage door to let Midnight out, "It's his home too. I won't have him all cooped up in his cage. It's been hard enough on him with all the moving around."

Midnight moved to climb out of the travel cage and stood on top of it. He leaned forward and kissed Brianna on her lips and happily said, *"Thank you, Momma!"*

Brianna smiled as she watched the little conure climb down onto the marble countertop, examining and tasting it with his tongue. From outside, Anna bellowed, "Lee! Jess! Get out here and help finish unloading the truck!"

"Coming dear," Lee answered cheerfully.

Both Lee and Jess moved in unison, but Brianna could hear her boyfriend mutter, "Why not include your damn daughter in your command?"

The witch scowled at him but then giggled as Midnight laughed as he watched the two men walk out the door. Brianna could always count on the little conure to brighten her mood and be the center of attention at any given moment. The witch walked over and dragged a couple of boxes that were labeled *kitchen* from the living area and into the kitchen, trying to organize the chaos that was her new home,

Lee and Jess were huffing and puffing as they dragged the wobbly queen mattress into the cabin while Anna carried the metal support frame with ease. Brianna looked to her mother, wanting to help, but got her mom's *don't you dare do it* gaze.

She felt guilty because she should be the one moving all the heavy stuff, it was hers after all.

She also knew, from the knowing glare Jess shot her as stormed back outside, that he was going to let her have it once her parents were gone.

"*Uh oh,*" Midnight spoke softly.

"You said it, bird, I'm in for one hell of a headache tonight." Brianna answered without looking at her feathered baby, but failed to notice that the conure was looking at one of the corners of the cabin, not at Jess.

Chapter Four

Daniel did his best to hide in the shadows, to observe the new occupants of *his* home. He might be dead but that didn't mean he was going to forfeit what he built with his own two hands many years ago. It wasn't like he had much of a choice. He was bound to this property due to the choices he made in the last days of his mortal life. The shadowy thing saw this as a cruel form of punishment.

The specter did what he could over the years to weaken the tether to his domicile, but each time it ended in failure. The shadowy thing always returned to mock him, reminding Daniel that his attempts were as pathetic as his attempt to save his family. It also forced Daniel to see visions of his family being mutilated and desecrated in unspeakable means, for his transgression.

Over the years, the specter made numerous attempts to warn the living about the dark presence that lurked nearby. Unfortunately, most never could see him, let alone hear his dire warnings. The shadowy thing didn't seem to care and was more amused by Daniel's actions.

They'll never acknowledge you. You will be dismissed as a figment of their imaginations, the shadowy thing mocked, adding to the specter's shame. *You couldn't save your pitiful family from me back then, what makes you think you can save my latest playthings now?*

Daniel only wanted to be reunited with his family, to ask them for their forgiveness in the role he played in their deaths. Every day that passed, he wept, knowing that this was his fate: to watch others suffer and die at the whims of the shadowy thing. Granted, the only ones that died here was him and his beloved family, the shadowy thing managed to *mark* the occupants so when they took their final breath on Earth, their souls would come directly to it.

The shadowy thing never stayed confined to the property, like the specter. It was free to move about and created terror and havoc elsewhere, especially when the cabin was vacant. Daniel didn't want to imagine how many other souls were damned to this infernal beast.

Their innocent blood is on my hands…

He wished that he had the power to destroy the shadowy thing, once and for all, so no one else would get hurt. In his mind, it was the only path he had to take for redemption, but the means of accomplishing this eluded him. He simply didn't have the power, something the shadowy thing had in copious amounts.

Daniel wasn't sure if he was capable of fighting. He could barely cause a picture on the wall to sway, so how could he manage an attack on a wicked creature of the darkness? The specter observed the people as they brought in more boxes, the amount of tension in the air was as thick and heavy as a muggy August day.

Daniel sighed, the constant bickering and negativity would be a beacon for the shadowy thing to feast on. Moving was stressful enough for people, but the raw emotions tended to fade once folks settled in. The specter had a feeling that it would get worse between the new occupants of the cabin. No amount of downtime would help this young couple. The infernal beast will be pleased with the new tenants.

The young male seemed self-absorbed and rude, like a petulant child. Daniel couldn't understand why this man-child was able to exist independently with the attitude he had, from what the otherworldly being had observed thus far. If this Jess were alive in Daniel's era, he would either lose that attitude or wouldn't be fed a meal until he earned it by doing a hard day's work or possibly some of his teeth.

Daniel could be wrong about him, but it would take a lot of evidence to change his mind after his first impression of this fellow. The specter would need to sit back in the shadows and observe the new occupants and figure out how to get them to leave for their own safety. The female seemed different from the other people that have lived here.

She had a strange glow about her that Daniel didn't quite recognize, but innately he understood the shine coming from her forehead: the woman was open and could *see* beings like him.

As exciting as this turn of events was, the ghost needed to be cautious. This Brianna did boast that she knew a few tricks to deal with unwanted spirits. She might get rid of him before Daniel could warn her about the shadowy thing and that wouldn't do. Is it possible that she might know how to get rid of the shadowy thing?

As much as the ghost wanted to latch on to this glimmer of hope, Daniel learned long ago that not much stood a chance against that malevolent creature. What's the point in getting his hopes up when the specter knew it would be crushed by his tormentor?

Daniel blended in with the natural shadows in the corners of the cabin with ease, they were his favorite hiding areas because he could mold his ethereal form to mimic his surroundings. He would be more obvious out in the open, but since people tended to put objects or large pieces of furniture to fill the spaces of corners, the shadow he cast could easily be dismissed.

These people didn't have much, but the ghost noticed that the couple had plenty of electrical items. He might be old, but Daniel learned by observation and knew that he could manipulate certain objects easier than others and electronics was one of his favorites.

Maybe he could communicate with this couple this way without freaking them out...much.

Daniel figured that this might backfire. It had in the past, causing the occupants to flee and never to return, but at least they were safe. If Brianna wouldn't listen to him, the ghost would resort to using electrical means because this couple's lives were in danger.

She had to listen, she *had* to!

Daniel resigned himself to waiting in the shadows for now. Nothing would come from trying to communicate, given the obvious stress from the move-in day. If anything, the ghost could wait until the couple fell asleep and attempt to converse with them in their dreams. It would be taxing on the couple, but with the danger that was waiting for them, it was the only option, Daniel reasoned.

The ghost wished that his cabin would burn down so no one else would become the shadowy thing's new plaything. Daniel was bound to the land, not the cabin, but he wished that he could leave or go to Heaven. If that was possible. Maybe he was in Hell and this was his eternal torture, with less fire and brimstone. Daniel chuckled softly, thinking of all he thought he knew in life. It didn't hold a cup of coffee to his crash course lessons during his afterlife.

The ghost found his spectral gaze kept focusing on the young lady as she came and went. As he observed her, Daniel could see she, despite the sweat and grime, was beautiful in every way possible. There was something about her that he couldn't get out of his mind. It frustrated the ghost.

Why am I so drawn to her?

Daniel's musing was interrupted by a screeching sound, coming from outside. Whatever it was, Daniel couldn't say, but when Brianna walked back in the cabin, she had a small cage in her arms.

The bird inside that cage made that terrible noise?

The ghost couldn't fathom how such a tiny creature could unleash an ear-piercing screech. Daniel may be dead, but he felt a nasty headache was in his future if this green feathered pet had more outbursts like that. What surprised Daniel more than that was that the bird could talk. It used short, choppy sentences like a three-year-old. Just like his own children did so long ago...

The bird locked its tiny eyes on Daniel and uttered, "*Uh oh.*"

The ghost sensed that this bird had an intelligence that belied its miniature stature. He could tell it saw him easily, which shocked the ghost. He had been seen by animals in the past, but never had one actually spoke to him. Was it afraid of him or was it trying to warn his owner of his presence?

Brianna didn't catch on to the bird's warning, brushing it off and thinking that this Midnight was referring to the cockroach named Jess. The bird kept watching the ghost intently, not saying another word.

Daniel noticed that his new avian sentinel also displayed a similar aura as Brianna, like the two of them were connected to each other somehow. The specter felt a flicker of excitement. Maybe this pet could help him communicate with the couple, if it was willing. Daniel decided to wait and observe the new occupants.

Chapter Five

The new couple sat at the dining table, with their respective parents, eating pizza and wings while drinking soda, using red Dixie cups. As peaceful as it appeared, the tension was thick in the room. Everyone was tired from the move; Brianna felt the brunt of the exertion. As she slowly took a bite, Jane looked around, sneering in disgust, "This place should have been torn down a long time ago."

Daniel moved closer so he could observe this strange family. He could feel the tension all day as stuff was brought into the cabin, but now everything was about to explode like a river breaking a dam.

"I agree," Jess quickly added, "I wish that there was a better place we could live, but *this* is what I have to look forward to, a dreary old log cabin."

"I still think you two should have searched harder," Jane eyed Brianna with contempt, "it's like you are satisfied with living a life of squalor. At least when I was your age, I had -"

"A cave?" Brianna snapped, not wanting to listen to the same broken message that Jess's mother droned on, "No, you had it all because times were easier and things didn't cost five to six figures, like now."

"They have a roof over their heads, dear," William spoke, trying to placate his wife, "and that's all that matters. It could have been a lot worse. They could be out on the streets."

"You know good and well that there wasn't much available," Anna chimed in, glaring at the portly woman, "If Jess could keep a job and be a responsible adult, we wouldn't be sitting in this cabin right now."

Jess was about to defend himself, but a sharp glance from Anna backed him down as she added, "It doesn't help that he failed to keep the bills paid on time, especially the rent, and now our kids have eviction notices attached to their names. This creates a red flag for management companies and landlords alike."

Jane huffed as she pointed an accusatory meaty finger at Brianna, "Don't lay all the blame on my boy when *she* is fully capable of helping out with the expenses. Brianna doesn't do anything, but stays at home and *never* lifts a finger to be responsible in any way. She's the one holding them back, holding Jess back from being successful!"

"Now see here, Jane -" Lee piped up, but Anna rested a hand on his leg, interrupting an incoming tirade. She balefully eyed Jane and stated calmly, but with an authoritative voice, "Brianna has a legitimate reason not to be working. It's called medical evidence, which is why she's on disability. If she wasn't in such bad health, she would run circles around all of us. Even on her worst days, which will be over the next week or so because of this move, Bri can do more around the house than Jess could ever do."

"At least my boy tries," Jane replied as she gazed at her son, "It's her job to take care of the house and him when he's the one bringing in the income."

"Have to keep a job for that to work," Brianna muttered under her breath. A giggle caught her attention. She glanced around at everyone in the room, trying to discern who heard her snark. Jess was stuffing a wing into his mouth with a smug affect. Jane and her parents were locked in a tense confrontation. William seemed to be ignored, but cast a sympathetic look at her.

So, who was it that laughed?

"If she wasn't the responsible one, their situation would be more dire," Anna answered as she poured herself some diet 7UP, "Brianna gets monthly disability checks. Less than eight hundred dollars. It isn't much, but at least it's a steady income, as opposed to no money when Jess gets himself fired. It's quite pathetic that a woman with all her health issues has to be the one expected to do *everything.* She's the one that makes sure the bills get paid and that they have enough food to live off."

"Obviously," Jane looked down her nose at Brianna, "she doesn't know how to do that since we are here in this dreadful place."

"You're so right, Jane," Brianna snapped as she defiantly jutted her chin out, "I'm so incompetent and lazy, that's it. It must be nice to not have to worry about money or if the bank account is still in the red because *someone* here lives beyond our means. I can't give him the money to pay the bills and expect him to do it because he will take it and buy the latest video game and fast food with it."

"I'm not like that," Jess challenged as he maliciously eyed his girlfriend, "You're just trying to make me sound like the bad guy in all of this. I'm a responsible guy."

"Yeah," Brianna retorted, pointing at the counter top by the sink, "I still have all the shut-off notices, the bounced check statements, failure to pay, and eviction notices that say otherwise in that box over there."

The specter moved to inspect the contents of the box that the young lady mentioned. He was curious if what she claimed was true. Being a ghost had its advantages at times, now was one of them. He was raised to respect his elders, men did all the hard labor to support the family, and women took care of the household, but as time passed, Daniel saw that this wasn't the mindset of others through the years.

Despite being dark in the box, the specter could see clearly and what he saw shocked him to his core. The words *past due* and *cutoff notice* stood out, stamped in big, bold red ink. The ghost shuffled the papers around the best he could, trying not to draw attention to his perusing. There were bank statements that showed accounts had insufficient funds, each one was at least three hundred dollars minimum.

How could this couple survive like this?

Daniel caught sight of an eviction notice, stating that they were two months behind on payments. The rental amount owed was three times what Brianna got monthly, meaning Jess wasn't living up to his claim of responsibility. *He was responsible*, the specter mused as he moved away from the box, glaring at the young man, *responsible for all the financial ineptitude.* Daniel hovered next to the young man and he mentally scoffed.

He's not worth being referred to as a man.

Jess was in the process of trying to drink and explain the contents of the box to everyone when Daniel used all his otherworldly strength and aimed for his hand. Moving papers was one thing, making physical contact took more effort and energy. Fueled by his rage, the specter hit the red cup so hard that it dislodged from Jess's hand and it struck him in the face, spilling the liquid contents all over him.

"Good boy!" Midnight shouted cheerfully.

Brianna paused for a moment and then she snorted as she laughed, which made Daniel happy. Jess glared as he stood up, soda dripping from his chin. Jane looked at her son, feeling mortified as she handed him several napkins, "Sweetie, you need to be a bit more careful with your drink. Clean yourself up now."

"I-I didn't do it," Jess whined, looking down at his plastic cup at his feet, "It felt like it was thrown at me. Like, really hard."

"Sure," Brianna jabbed as she grinned, "and are you sure that the ghost did it and not just you being clumsy? Maybe Casper didn't like your explanation."

"Something did it to me and now I'm a soaking wet mess. It broke the cup too, look for yourself!" Jess adamantly stated, as he grabbed his cup off the floor. He threw it at Brianna, hitting her in the chest, as he stormed out of the room to change clothes. As he passed Midnight's cage, the bird chirped up, *"Bad Daddy!"*

"Jerk!" Both Brianna and Daniel spat out simultaneously.

Jane stood up from her chair and ordered, "I'll go check on him. William, go start the car. We're leaving this place."

As Jane ambled her heavy form towards the bedroom, William stood up, nodding. He grabbed several slices of pizza and wrapped them in paper towels. As he walked to the front door, he paused and put a hand on Brianna's shoulder and spoke with a genuinely warm demeanor, "I'm sorry about their antics. You have a lovely new home. I hope you two will be happy here, no matter what."

"Thanks William," Brianna smiled as the man walked out the door. She tore a few pieces of crust off the end of her pizza and walked over to Midnight. As she placed the bread into the food dish, Midnight bobbed his head several times, "*Thanks. Midnight love Momma!*"

"We better do the same dear," Lee commented, "It will be a long drive back home and if we leave now, we might beat most of the Portland traffic out of here."

"Wait," Brianna gasped in surprise, "you're leaving town tonight? I thought you were going to spend the night at a motel first?"

"We were," Anna replied, feeling a bit deflated, "but your father overruled me on this. I'm tired and done arguing for one night."

Brianna rushed over and gave her mother a hug goodbye and said to her father, "You got cheap, didn't you?"

"You know it's expensive here," Lee replied, trying to justify his reasoning, "and with the move, money is tight all around. We would stay, but we can't afford it."

Anna squeezed her daughter as she whispered in her ear, "You're both right. As much as I would like to stay and help you get this place unpacked, we must go. I love you, dear."

Brianna's dad came up and hugged her as soon as she let go of Anna. The two walked out the front door and Anna called back over her shoulder, "Call me if you need anything."

"I will. I love you both!" Brianna replied, wondering when she would see them again. Her parents live in Clarkston, Washington, an eight-hour drive one way from Portland and that's with light traffic. She stood on the porch and waved at her parents as they left down the pothole path. Brianna hugged herself as Jane stepped next to her. She sneered as she spoke, "Squalor suits you perfectly, Brianna, not my son."

"Then take him with you if you don't like the idea of him living here!"

"I can't. For some reason, he wants to remain here, with *you*. I can't force him to do anything. You have your claws in my son and will always hold him back. You are so selfish, child! I hope Jess comes to his senses in time before you totally ruin him."

Before Brianna could reply, Jane walked away. She watched Jess's mother waddle her way to her luxury car where her husband waited behind the wheel, waving goodbye with a smile. Jane opened the car door and before she shimmied into the passenger seat, the ghost appeared behind the portly woman. He grabbed two handfuls of her hair and violently yanked back, causing the heavy-set woman to drop hard on the ground.

William gasped as he hopped out the car and ran over to help out his wife. Brianna trotted over to help the cantankerous woman up, trying to hide an amused smile. William and the witch both hooked their arms under her armpits, guiding her to a sitting position.

Jane glared as she rubbed the back of head as William asked, "Are you okay, dear? What happened?"

She pointed an accusatory finger at Brianna, "This little shit is what happened! She just assaulted me!"

"What!" Brianna incredulously blurted out, "I didn't do this!"

"Yes, you did! I felt your cold fingers grab my beautiful hair and knocked me down."

"Sweetheart," William soothingly spoke as he assisted his wife to her feet, "Brianna didn't do this. She was up on her porch when you fell. She was nowhere near us, let alone you, my dear."

She shook Brianna's hands off her flabby arm as she hoisted herself up, using the car door to get her balance. Jane glared at Brianna, her eyes narrowed as she growled, "I know what I felt, dear. Hands in my hair! I know it was *her*!"

"I'm sure you did feel that, but Brianna wasn't the culprit."

Brianna smirked as she taunted Jane, "Maybe it was the evil ghost that attacked you. Perhaps it doesn't appreciate your mean attitude."

Jane gritted her teeth as she angrily growled, "Take me home, William."

"Yes, dear." He answered as Jane slumped down in the car seat. He closed the door and gave Brianna a sympathetic smile, "It's okay. It was probably just a misstep on her part. I know you had nothing to do with it."

The witch hugged him and said, "I know. I'm just tired and I need rest, not another argument over something I didn't do. Have a safe trip home, William."

Jane rolled down her window and scoffed, "William, now!"

He walked around the front of the luxury car, smiling and waving at Brianna. Jane glared at her as her window rolled back up, muttered to herself. Brianna ignored Jess's mother as they turned the car around and went down the dirt path.

Daniel stood silently near her, wondering if he upset the witch. He could tell from the few discussions that there was a lot of tension between her and Jess and his mother. He didn't like the way that they treated her, like she was beneath them for some reason.

He observed this woman as she walked slowly around on the property, not wanting to go back inside. Brianna wrapped her arms around her chest. She cried as she shook her head. Daniel hung back just enough that she wouldn't notice him, but close enough to hear what she said to herself.

"Why do I let them get to me?" Brianna asked as tears streamed down her soft cheeks, hiccupping quick breaths. She was taught by the women in her family to be strong and unfazed by stress in the presence of others. Only when privacy was possible was when breaking down was allowed. All of the pain from unloading the moving truck and emotional stress culminated in her current release.

"Squalor? That woman wouldn't know squalor if it sprouted out of her ass!" Brianna fumed as she kicked a rock from her path. The ghost felt a strong urge to hold and comfort her. She might be a witch, but Brianna didn't deserve the treatment she had just endured. No one did.

Brianna looked at her new cabin, took a deep breath, and marched towards it, ready to deal with Jess. She figured that he would still be moody about his glass breaking on him. Brianna wondered if the ghost had a hand in it, but it didn't matter because Jess's anger will be focused on her alone.

She stepped up onto the porch and slowly walked inside. Jess watched her as he sat down behind his computer, grumbling, "When you get up in the morning, can you call and get the internet hooked up?"

"I can, but why can't you," Brianna answered.

"I'm going to be busy."

"Doing what exactly? Job hunting, I hope." Brianna bitterly spat.

"No, I need my rest." Jess grumbled as he played a pinball game on his computer, "All this heavy lifting today has my back aching. I'm going to need some downtime before I go job hunting."

Brianna rolled her eyes, "Yet another excuse."

Jess quickly stood up and got in Brianna's face, towering over her, "If you got something to say, then say it. I tire of your snark."

"Yes, the truth hurts, doesn't it?" Brianna stated as she poked him on his chest, "Your laziness is what's got us in so much hot water lately that I can't tell if we will have a roof over our heads from day to day."

"So, me not calling the internet company makes me lazy in your eyes?" Jess huffed as he dramatically threw his arms up in the air in frustration, "Figures. I can't do anything right in your eyes, can I?"

"Damn right. There's a box over there that pretty much sums up your inability to be a mature, responsible adult. If it wasn't for me and what little disability money I get, as well as my website building jobs that I can get, we would be in a lot worse shape!"

Jess sneered as he roughly grabbed Brianna's arm as he retorted with contempt, "I'd say go find someone else to be with or, better yet, go live on your own. We both know that you can't afford it on your paltry monthly income. Face it, *babe*. You're stuck with me, whether you like it or not."

Brianna yanked her arm free and rubbed it as Jess stormed back over to his computer and sat down. Midnight angrily cried out, *"Bad daddy! No ow momma!"*

Jess snarled at the bird, "Then tell momma to treat me right."

Midnight dug around in his food dish, grabbed out a walnut, and with the precision of an Army sniper, threw it at Jess. It hit him on his temple, causing Jess to yelp. He glared at the conure and demanded, "Why did you do that! You know I hate it when you throw things at me!"

"Bad daddy!" Midnight shouted as he puffed up. He leaned forward and yanked at the door latch, wanting out. Jess stood up and stormed to the bedroom.

He waded up and tossed a piece of paper at the cage, further antagonizing the bird, and coldly stated, "I'm going to bed. You deal with *your* damn bird and get in here."

"He's your bird too," Brianna retorted, "I don't know when I'll be coming to bed but-"

"For fuck's sake, Bri!" Jess frustratingly yelled, "Either sleep with me or out here! I don't care, just pick. I'm tired and I'm going to bed."

Brianna meekly turned her head and flinched as he slammed the door shut. All was quiet in the cabin. She walked over and opened Midnight's cage door.

"*Momma okay, please?*" The bird asked as Brianna leaned down next to him.

"I'm okay, baby," Brianna cooed. She stood there, kissing his shiny black beak, "Momma is tired. We're all tired, even you, mister."

Daniel watched as the woman put her hand on the bird's back. It kept rubbing its beak against Brianna's cheeks while softly chattering. The ghost unknowingly moved closer, catching the attention of the conure. It eyed Daniel closely before moving away from Brianna and announced, "*Hi, good boy!*"

Brianna turned around and searched everywhere. She didn't see anyone there, so she asked, "Who are you talking to, Midnight?"

The conure repeatedly bobbed his head in excitement, "*Good boy! Step up! Step up!*"

Daniel leaned down next to Midnight's cage while Brianna kept her back to them.

"*Good boy!*"

"Is someone here, baby?"

Midnight curved his head inward, his way of nonverbally answering yes. Brianna closed the cage door and locked it, much to the bird's dismay. She walked around quietly, knowing that there weren't many spots for a person to hide in the small cabin.

Unless it wasn't a living person.

Daniel moved past the cage, causing the bird to cry out in excitement, "*Look! Pretty boy, here!*"

Brianna turned around and saw no one, just an excited bird. Muffled slightly by the closed door, Jess cried out from the bedroom, "Hurry up and put that bird night-night. He's keeping me awake!"

"Fine," Brianna answered as she rolled her eyes. She looked around the living room and found Midnight's blue cover for his cage. As she draped it over the cage, Brianna whispered, "Night night, Midnight. Night night, pretty boy. Have sweet dreams and be a good boy tomorrow. I love you, Midnight. I love you, pretty boy."

"Love momma!" The conure whispered as the blue cloth fell in place.

Brianna smiled as she backed away. She looked around again at the cabin and announced, "I know that you're here. If you wish to stay, you need to behave. I'm going to cleanse my house tomorrow. I don't need any negative entities in my life," she eyed the bedroom door and added, "Gods know that I have plenty of negativity as it is."

She heard no reply.

Brianna slumped her shoulders as she slowly walked towards the bedroom, each step was erratic and a struggle. Daniel could see the pain coming to the forefront on her sweat coated visage.

The ghost attempted to open the door for her, but didn't have enough energy for it. It was infuriating to him that he couldn't do more. His power seemed to be stronger when his emotions were put behind it. The specter was drained from his antics tonight, Daniel needed to recover in the hopes that he can somehow communicate with this female.

Brianna opened the door and padded quietly as she could without disturbing Jess, who was snoring away. The ghost hovered in the corner, wanting to watch over her as she slept. If the shadowy thing returned, Daniel would make it his mission to protect this Brianna from harm.

Jess, not so much.

That creature can have the little whelp.

He watched as the woman pulled off her shirt, exposing her breasts, and tossed it on the floor. Brianna used her feet to kick off her shoes and then tugged off her black ankle socks. She grimaced in pain as she bent over and peeled off her pants, letting them pool at her feet.

As Brianna stood up, the ghost let out an ethereal gasp of approval. She was beautiful and had many curvy features that he could appreciate. Her skin was creamy white, with the exception of the red patches burned by the sun, others from exertion from moving here.

Of all the people that have come and gone from his house, this woman seemed perfect to him. Her breasts hypnotically heaved with each breath, her core looked warm and inviting.

She turned and sat down on the side of the bed, reaching for medicine bottles that sat on a box that doubled as a nightstand. With pills in hand, Brianna hugged herself as she shook her head. She groaned as she stood back up and gingerly walked out of the bedroom, looking for something to drink.

She made her way to the table and opened a two liter of root beer. Brianna popped the medicine in her mouth and drank straight from the bottle. The ghost observed that she was in a great deal of pain and yet, she had to fend for herself. He glared at her sleeping boyfriend, *"You should do your job and care for this woman!"*

He rushed over and hovered over the guy and, as hard as he could, smacked Jess on the side of his face. The strike caused Jess to startle awake, just as Brianna walked into the room.

"What's wrong?"

Jess rubbed his face softly, looking confused as he sat up, "I don't know. It feels like I just got slapped."

Brianna cautiously looked around and said, "Are you sure? I don't see anyone else in here, but you."

"Are you calling me a liar?" He snarled as he pointed at his cheek, "Does this look fake to you, Bri?"

"I never said it was," she huffed, "I'm just saying that there's nothing around that could have done it."

"It was probably you," Jess sneered as he rolled over onto the side, "You would hit me when I can't defend myself."

"I would never do that," Brianna protested with her hands on her hips, "I'd wait for you to be awake and in front of me. I'm not a coward that attacks while you sleep."

"Shut your mouth and get your fat ass in bed, damn it!" Jess bellowed as he yanked the blanket over his body. Brianna rolled her eyes as she struggled to get back to bed, a single tear trickled down her soft cheek.

She whimpered as she lay down on her side of the bed, barely covering her naked form. Daniel hovered next to her and managed to muster up enough energy to move the covers over her body, tucking her in.

"Thank you," Brianna murmured softly with her eyes closed, holding the blanket tightly.

Daniel smiled as he moved away so he wouldn't disturb her rest.

Chapter Six

The next day, Brianna woke up, both stiff and sore, alone in her queen size bed. She sat up and grimaced in pain. Brianna was not only feeling all the pain from the moving day, but her fibromyalgia had her body screaming in agony.

She got dressed in a long cotton nightgown and walked stiffly to the door, hoping that Jess had made breakfast. She smelled something that had her stomach rumbling. She opened the door and saw that he had made scrambled eggs and toast.

The pan was covered in reminiscence of fried yokes coating the sides. Grunting caused her to look over her shoulder. Jess was at his desk, hooking cords up to his tower while on his side.

"Did you save me any food?" Brianna asked as she meandered over to the refrigerator, knowing the answer that was coming.

"I'm afraid not, babe," Jess shouted from under the desk, "I didn't know when you would be up, so I fed myself."

Bri nodded as she grabbed out a carton of eggs and a bag of shredded cheese. She grabbed a different skillet and sat it on the burner. Bri crinkled her nose in disgust at the utter mess that he made on the once pristine clean flat range top.

Guess I'll be cleaning today…

Brianna turned on the burner as she sprayed Pam in the skillet before cracking two eggs in it. As she mixed the eggs, Brianna called out, "Did you find my computer while you've been out here today?"

Exacerbated, Jess replied, "Yes, it's over in the corner by the front window. Did you want me to hook it up?"

"Yes, please," Brianna answered as she sprinkled the shredded cheese and folded it in, along with salt and pepper. She turned around to the small island and grabbed a paper plate and spooned her breakfast on it.

She walked over and sat down at the dinner table. Too exhausted to get back up for a glass of milk, Brianna reached over and grabbed the bottle of root beer and poured some into one of the red Solo cups on the table. Jess scooted out from under his desk and walked over to Brianna. He kissed her on the cheek as he reached down and snatched some of her eggs in his fingertips. He stuffed it into his mouth as he walked over to set up Brianna's computer.

The witch sighed as she dipped her fork into her food. She had a lot of work to do and knew that Jess wouldn't be any help. He shuffled boxes around and unburied Brianna's desk and quickly set it up. As he turned it on, his cellphone rang. Jess looked at the ID and saw that it was an IT company in downtown Portland.

"Hello? Yes, speaking." Brianna listened intently to the one-sided conversation, "I can be there in thirty minutes. Sounds good. I'll see you then. Thanks. Goodbye."

"Good news?" Brianna asked.

"I have an interview with Corridor IT in," Jess answered, beaming a smile, as he looked at his watch, "forty-five minutes. I'm going to change and head out."

"That's great. I hope you get it."

"Yeah, we will see how it goes," Jess replied as he rushed past her and into the main bedroom. Brianna's excitement ebbed by his reply. He needed a job, but he tends to turn his nose up at most offers for his IT skills. The witch wished that Jess would accept the position and stick with it.

Unconsciously, she glanced at the box of unpaid bills, and sighed as she took another bite of her cheesy eggs. The stress of not having extra money weighed heavily on her shoulders because Jess didn't think about the repercussions of constantly losing employment.

The ghost sat back and observed her, seeing that her sadness still showed. He saw her boyfriend run out of the bedroom and asked, "Can I get some money from you? I want to pick up some groceries when I finish my interview."

"No, but you can take my EBT card and use it for groceries."

Jess groaned, "I'd rather have cash, babe."

"I'm sure you would, but the last few times I gave you cash, you spent it on games and junk food instead of on the bills it was intended for in the first place."

"I don't need your flack right now," Jess growled, "I'm going to the store so give me the damn card."

Brianna sighed as she pointed at her wallet on the counter, "It's in there, just open the flap and take it."

Jess grumbled as he opened it up and slipped out the EBT card. He eyed the cash inside, but as Brianna cleared her throat, he sat her wallet back down and walked towards the front door. Brianna sighed, *why does everything have to be a fight?*

The witch finished her breakfast off and hobbled over to the sink and got the dirty dishes soaking. She grabbed a wet sponge and scrubbed at the caked-on food spatter that Jess made on the stove top. She glanced over her shoulder and smiled as she heard the conure rattling the lock on his cage.

"You wanna come see momma?"

Midnight quickly bobbed his head as Brianna uncovered him, *"Yes! Help momma!"*

She waited patiently for the bird to have his first bowel movement of the day, not wanting to be covered in a heap of poop. Brianna had plenty of things to do today, items to go through, but the number one priority was to work on the queue of websites to build.

Midnight released a slurry of green and white poop. Brianna unfastened the lock on the cage door and he hopped out and climbed up onto her shoulder. As they slowly made their way over to her PC, the witch grimaced the whole way. Gingerly, she sat down in her leather swivel chair and turned on her computer.

Midnight rubbed his black beak against Brianna's cheek as she opened one of the files that she'd been working on for the last two weeks. It was difficult to get anything done with all the stress and turmoil of recent events. Just for once, the witch wished that Jess would grow up and be the responsible one.

Why does it have to fall on me?

She buried her face in her hands and sobbed. Jess knew that it wasn't good for her health, but he didn't seem to care. Bills got paid eventually so why not buy the more expensive games was his reasoning during one of their many heated arguments.

Midnight kissed her on her cheek and softly spoke, "*No cry, momma. Kiss kiss all right?*"

"Momma's okay. You don't have to worry about me."

The conure climbed down onto Brianna's chest and eyed her intently. She could see that the little bird was trying to determine if this was true. Brianna looked back at the computer screen and typed in more coding. Midnight nuzzled his black head and beak against her neck, chattering softly.

The conure was the only bright side of her relationship with Jess. They were asked by a veterinarian in Lake Oswego if they would be willing to take in the conure. Brianna had been around the bigger birds growing up and was hoping to find a Rose Breasted Cockatoo.

Brianna was reluctant at first, since she had never taken care of a conure before, but the little bird's backstory simply melted her reservations. The vet said that her office got a call about a parrot insistently trying to get into a house. The doctor went to catch the wayward bird and right away, knew that something was off. The woman who called about the bird had all the proper food, supplies, and a cage perfect for Midnight's size, but insisted that he wasn't hers.

The vet talked to the neighbors and was told that the conure was tossed outside and any time the bird tried to get back in the house, the woman used a broom to smack it away. Midnight was both malnourished, underweight, and traumatized, which made it difficult to find the bird a better home. No one wanted to take on the burden, but with one look into the conure's little black eyes, the witch had to take him in.

The vet was so relieved that she tossed in a cage and some bird supplies for free. Midnight was quiet and reserved for the first two weeks and then he screeched loudly. Both Brianna and Jess understood why the vet had trouble finding this bird a home. The conure was more attached to Jess in the beginning, but as time went on, Midnight bonded with Brianna as the constant fighting grew.

The bird got more aggressive towards Jess, especially when he caused his momma to cry, which was becoming more frequent. As Brianna worked, the ghost came closer. He was curious about what she was doing, but for the unlife of him, Daniel couldn't figure it out.

All he saw on the screen was a bunch of numbers, symbols, and words. The ghost was scratching his head and didn't notice that the little green bird was staring at him until it spoke, "*Momma. Pretty boy here!*"

Brianna paused her typing and slowly looked around, but saw no one. She grimaced in pain as she turned around in her chair and said, "Okay, whomever you are, I can't see or hear you at the moment. The pain is blocking it out, but I do acknowledge your presence. Just know that it might be a little while before we can have a two-way conversation. I'm going to cleanse and bless the cabin eventually. My name is Brianna and I'm a

Witch, as well as a Warrior of Gaia, and this little fella here is Midnight, my familiar. All I ask is that you don't cause any problems here. If you do, I won't hesitate to forcefully move you on. Do we have an understanding?"

Daniel wasn't sure what to make of this woman. He wasn't exactly sure what she meant by being a Warrior of Gaia, but the ghost knew more about witches.

At least, Daniel thought he did.

The specter looked directly at the bird and nodded as he replied, "*I understand. I won't cause any problems for her. Can you convey my message, Midnight?*"

Midnight eyed him, Daniel could see the bird was thinking, and the bird bobbed his head several times.

"Does he agree, Midnight?"

"*He's a good boy!*" The conure excitedly shouted. The bird climbed up on Brianna's shoulder, puffed up, and sternly said to the ghost, "*My momma! Midnight love momma!*"

Brianna smiled at her bird as she shook her head, "Midnight is protective of me. Are you the one that's been running people off from this cabin?"

"*Yes...and no,*" Daniel replied and waited for the bird to translate.

The conure gave a quick nod and then said, "*No momma.*"

Brianna looked puzzled by what the conure did so she asked, "What do you mean by *no*? I saw you nod for yes. Is there something else living here?"

"*Yes!*" Daniel replied, excited that the lady might heed his warning, "*A shadowy creature that's roaming the area lives here and has me trapped! Tell her, bird - I mean Midnight, please!*"

Midnight looked at his momma and gave her another quick head nod and said, "*Yes! Bad boy!*"

Brianna rubbed her forehead, grimacing as the pain as the fibromyalgia reminded her of overdoing it the past few days. Concentration was going to be difficult, especially trying to code while attempting to decipher what the conure was relaying.

"I need to get some work done," Brianna bit out as she stood up. The witch painfully shuffled towards the bedroom, snatching the bottle of root beer, "Just behave and we will be fine. I'm not in the mood for an ornery ghost."

She entered the bedroom and walked over and grabbed an orange pill bottle. Brianna panted slightly as she unscrewed the lid and said, "I know that it was you that attacked both Jess and his mother last night. If you try to harm me, I *will* ensure that you won't enjoy being shredded."

Daniel hovered next to her as she took a couple of white pills and swallowed them. The specter placed an ethereal hand on her shoulder and said while looking at the conure, *"I will never cause you an ounce of pain or grief, Brianna."*

"Good boy, momma," Midnight stated as Brianna stood up, wincing in pain as she moved. She nodded as she shambled back to her computer, carrying a two liter with her.

Brianna sat down and pecked away at the keys on the keyboard.

The ghost pushed his way through the wall and went outside. For some reason, he didn't fear this young woman, even though she was a witch. In the short time that the new owners of his cabin were here, Daniel felt compelled to protect and watch over her.

Brianna may be the one who could reunite him with his family, but he wasn't sure if they were in Heaven or if the shadowy thing had devoured their souls. One thing that Daniel knew for certain is that he needed to be more vigilant.

If need be, I'll gladly let that thing destroy me before I allow it to harm her.

Chapter Seven

Jess returned from his interview, carrying several bags of groceries in his hands as he flung the front door open. He strolled past Brianna and sat the bags down on the countertop. He walked over, tossed the EBT card on her desk and kissed Brianna on the cheek.

She glanced over at him and asked, "How did the interview go?"

"It went well as to be expected," Jess flatly stated as he straightened up, stretching with his arms over his head, "They want me to work on the graveyard shift, monitoring their new printers and recording any kind of issues as they run."

Brianna could already tell that he didn't want it so she asked, "Did you accept the offer? How much are they offering?"

"The pay isn't nearly as much as I deserve. I told them that I will have to think about it and let them know if I want the job or not," Jess replied as if he was bored.

Brianna swiveled around in her chair to face her boyfriend and demanded, "It doesn't matter if you want it or not. We need the income so call them and take it."

"They're trying to start me out at a barely entry salary," Jess whined as he pulled out a wadded-up piece of paper and handed it to her, "I have the experience that requires them to pay me a higher rate. Not this laughable offer."

Brianna eyed him, "Really? After everything we've just gone through, you're going to be picky?"

Jess sneered, "I have standards so-"

Brianna snorted, "Yeah and you've had jobs that offered you better pay and you still managed to squander those opportunities by calling in sick too often just because you stayed up late playing WoW."

Jess leaned down and got in Brianna's face and coldly snarled as he roughly squeezed her arms, "At least I'm trying, which is more than I can say about you, Bri. All you ever do is sit around the house, bitching and complaining. Maybe you should spend more of your efforts into your side business and less time criticizing me. I'm tired of carrying the financial burden in this relationship."

Brianna grimaced, "Let go. You're hurting me!"

As Brianna cried out in pain, Midnight lunged as he yelled, *"Bad daddy! No ow momma?"*

The conure bit down on Jess's hand hard, piercing his skin and drawing blood. Jess recoiled, holding his hand and glaring at the bird, "Ouch! Stupid bird!"

Midnight perched up on Brianna's shoulder and puffed up with his black beak open, *"Midnight ow daddy! My momma!"*

Jess stormed off to leave, yelling, "I'm heading back into town since I'm not wanted here. Keep your bird on a tight leash if you know what's for both of you."

He slammed the door as Brianna muttered, "Asshole."

She got up and stiffly meandered over to Midnight's cage. Brianna struggled to get the conure to go back into his cage. The bird kept kissing her on the cheek and repeatedly asked, *"Momma okay, please?"*

"Momma's okay. I'm going to go for a walk. Be a good boy and get back in your cage."

Midnight's eyes brightened with excitement as he shouted, *"Midnight go bye bye with momma!"*

"Not right now, baby," Brianna countered as she pressed her shoulder into the opening of the cage, trying to coax the conure to go in, "Momma needs some alone time. Please get in your cage."

Midnight grumbled incoherently as he reluctantly hopped on the perch. The bird turned around and stretched out for kisses. Brianna smiled as she leaned forward and pursed her lips and let him repeatedly kiss them. The witch stood up and closed and locked the cage door.

Brianna walked over to the couch and slipped on her shoes. She grabbed her MP3 player and connected it to a small speaker and said, "Do you want music to listen to?"

"*Yes, please!*" Midnight chirped up, bobbing his head.

Brianna gingerly walked towards the door and replied, "Momma will be back shortly. You be a good boy."

The witch stepped outside and slowly walked down the dirt path as tears streamed down her face. It seemed like a good time, now that Jess wasn't around, to break down and let her emotions flow out like the water in the creek.

The sound of her whimpering caught Daniel's attention. He followed nearby, trying his best not to be noticed. The specter took one look at her and could tell that she and her boyfriend had been fighting again.

Brianna was holding her arms under her ample breasts tightly, her breaths coming in quick succession. Daniel's anger flared as he observed her in this emotional turmoil.

So, help me, I will strangle that boy when he returns!

Brianna walked along the bank, listening to the running water. She didn't understand why Jess was being so entitled. She could see him not liking the hourly rate, but in their current situation, any wage was better than nothing at all. It's not like the company wouldn't give him a raise if he stayed there long enough. Jess could look for a higher paying job while working for this IT company so what was the problem?

Brianna found a nice spot to sit down and relax. A large pine tree towered close to the creek bank and had a big enough crook at its base that she could wedge her body in like a cozy alcove. She sat down on a patch of moss that grew at the base of the tree and kicked off her shoes.

Brianna slid her feet into the creek, letting the cool running water relax her. She closed her eyes and let out a long breath. Daniel watched her body visibly relax as her breathing slowed down as Brianna slipped into a meditative state. He was mesmerized by her plump breasts, watching them move in tandem with each inhalation. Daniel could see her body physically relaxing and it looked like she was peacefully sleeping.

Brianna let out a soft sigh of content, "I needed this. Nature therapy is good for the soul. Why can't life be this enjoyable?"

"It would be without that little child you call a boyfriend," Daniel replied, oozing with snark.

"I have no choice in the matter," Brianna replied with a shrug, her eyes still closed, "I can't afford to live here on my own. My medical conditions prevent me from having a normal job and a life."

Daniel's eyes widened with excitement as he realized that this woman could now hear him. He squatted down beside her and asked, *"What ailments hinder you, Bri?"*

Brianna snorted, "Too many to count. The main ones are fibromyalgia and chronic fatigue."

The ghost looked at her with curiosity and asked, *"I'm not familiar with those? What are they?"*

Brianna sadly sighed, "So few do. Most doctors don't believe that it's a real disease so they will prescribe the usual default treatment of eating healthy and exercise daily and that will cure it because *it's all in my head*. Doctors don't understand it and are unable to classify it. It's like every single nerve in my body is at war with me. I'm in constant pain with no relief in sight. Not even my pain pills can make it lessen."

"That doesn't sound pleasant. What makes it worse?"

"Physical exertion, stress, doing more than I should without pacing myself. My doctor won't allow me to work unless I can find a job that will allow me to work at my own pace with plenty of breaks and set my own schedule. I'm trying to start my own business creating websites, but it's slow going when no one knows you exist in this big world."

"Is pain and fatigue the only issues? I only ask because I can see inside you and can't tell what else is happening in your beautiful damaged body."

Brianna was about to answer, but a sharp laugh escaped her lips. Then it occurred to her that she was talking to the otherworldly inhabitant of her new cabin. The witch focused with her third eye without opening her eyelids and could plainly see him.

The specter was dressed in a weather-worn button shirt and had on soiled pants that reeked of being a farmer. His face had the telltale signs of a tan, despite being pale. He had thick, dark hair and eyes that matched. Brianna could sense a fair amount of sadness and bitterness from this entity so she asked, "Are you here to tell me your story so that you can move on from here?"

"No, I'm trying to warn you to leave this place. It isn't safe for you and the child that lays with you at night."

Brianna smiled warmly at the ghost's description of Jess. *Even the dead can tell that he's not a reliable guy,* the witch mused and then she asked, "What's your name?"

"Daniel Powell, my lady."

"Are you the one that attacked Jess last night," Brianna asked but felt like she already knew the answer.

The ghost was quick to respond, "*Yes and I'll do it again if he doesn't get his act together. You deserve a man that can treat you right and love you properly. He's a boy pretending to be a man. Um, may I ask you a question?*"

"Sure."

"*How is it that you can hear me now? Earlier, you told me that you couldn't. What's changed, my fair lady?*"

Brianna took in a deep breath, relishing in the tranquility of her new property, "If I can get my body to relax, the pain ebbs and with it, my third eye and hearing returns. Why do you linger here? I can help you move on, if you wish."

"*I'm trapped here by the very thing that I'm trying to warn you about. A shadowy thing, I'm not sure what it is, roams the area. It loves to cause strife and somehow attaches itself to others to torment. You must flee from here before it takes you...like it took me and my family.*"

Brianna smiled slightly, causing Daniel to growl, *"Does that amuse you, witch? I screwed up and we paid the price for it!"*

"No, but I'm not worried about your little dark captor. As I said before, I'm not only a witch but a Warrior of Gaia. It means that I'm ready to fight any nasty creature that roams the area."

"But it's too strong. I don't think that you can do it alone," the ghost pleaded, hoping that she would see reason.

Brianna chuckled, "I never said that I would be alone."

At that moment, several growls caught Daniel by surprise. He quickly turned around and saw a small pack of wolves of various sizes circling him. They weren't corporeal, more like the ghost, except more solid.

The biggest of the pack got between Daniel and Brianna. It stood up and took on a more humanoid form but was still a wolf. Daniel put his hands up in surrender, hoping that the wolves wouldn't attack.

"Daniel, I'd like for you to meet my pack. The big one is called SilverWolf and he's the alpha of the spirit wolves." Brianna stated.

"Is this ghost causing you pain?" SilverWolf asked, growling as he towered over the specter, *"The pack hasn't had a good fight and we would be glad to rid you of his presence."*

"No, he's alright. Daniel has it out for Jess, but he also claims that there's a dark entity lurking nearby."

"What creature is it," SilverWolf growled protectively.

The specter thought for a moment, still feeling intimidated by the spirit wolves, and then said, *"I'm not sure what it is exactly. It killed me and my family long ago and it loves tormenting any who reside here or the surrounding area. I do know that it was conjured by a witch."*

"When was the last time you saw it?" Brianna asked.

"It's been a few months. The shadowy thing enjoys returning here to torment me and telling me about all of its misdeeds." Daniel heavily sighed, feeling dejected and helpless, *"I couldn't stop it*

in life and I'm not strong enough to fight it in my current situation."

SilverWolf turned to the pack and commanded, "*Spread out and search the area. The hunt is on,*" as he got back on all fours, the wolf said, "*If it shows up, call for us and we will help you destroy it.*"

The spirit wolves split off and covered the grounds faster than any living wolves could do.

Chapter Eight

Daniel was transfixed on the young woman once more. He enjoyed watching her rhythmic breathing, mesmerized by her ample breasts beneath her cotton sleepshirt. The ghost had the urge to reach out and caress her cheek. His touch caused a little gasp to escape from Brianna's lips.

"You deserve better," Daniel softly spoke.

"You're probably right, but it's difficult to find someone better when you're in my physical condition."

"Why is this?"

Brianna sighed as she opened her eyes, "No one wants to deal with all my health issues. I'm seen as a burden and can't help financially either. If you were alive, I'm sure that you would feel the same."

Daniel's ethereal mouth dropped open, *"How can you lump me in that category? I'm not like most men you know. I would gladly care for you if I were alive."*

"You say that now," Brianna replied with a snort, "but you don't even know me or what I'm like to be around."

Daniel reached out and cupped one hand on the witch's cheek and gently caressed her other cheek, causing Brianna to gasp, "*You have a point, but know that I see more than you realize. I may be dead, but that doesn't mean that I can't care for you in my own way.*"

The witch closed her eyes, expecting her lips to be brushed with his wispy lips, but it didn't happen. She opened her eyes and saw that he was watching her with a hint of a smile. Brianna looked at the stream and asked, "Is it safe to go in there?"

Daniel never took his eyes off the woman and said, "*It's safe, at this moment.*" He cocked his head to the side and asked, "*Why do you ask?*"

The witch smiled mischievously as she grabbed the hem of her sleepshirt. Slowly, she tugged it over her head and neatly folded it. As she bent over to place it on the patch of moss, she heard the ghost let out a sigh of appreciation.

Brianna sauntered towards the edge of the stream and said over shoulder with a playful smile, "I'm going for a swim. Care to join me, Daniel?"

The witch stepped gingerly into the water, letting her body acclimate to its cool temperature. She gathered some water in her hands and let it cascade down her chest slowly. Brianna observed that her otherworldly friend was gawking in awe. She smiled as she motioned for Daniel to join her.

She felt his presence next to her as she laid down and floated on her back and asked with her eyes closed, "Do you see anything you like, Daniel?"

The ghost rubbed his hand over his ethereal mouth, feeling like his mouth was parched and at a loss for words. The natural rays from the sun kissed her pale freckled skin, glistening as the water lapped over her.

The ghost managed to speak once again in a hesitant way, *"Bri?"*

"Yes?"

"Um, with your permission...may I touch you?"

Brianna couldn't prevent the smile from happening. It was sweet that he asked and he almost sounded like a young man with a woman for the first time. She bit the inside of her cheek, curious as to how he would touch her.

Sex was practically non-existent in her relationship with Jess, especially the past few years. He didn't take care of himself which had his diabetes out of control, leading to a flaccid member that never stood erect. The only time he was able to get it up was by being rough with Brianna, especially during bondage. She was okay with it at first, but lately Jess had been bordering on abuse.

Daniel ran his translucent hands over Brianna's abdomen, causing her to shiver. With each swipe of his hands, Brianna let out a soft moan as she bit her bottom lip. The specter swirled his fingers over her ample breasts, causing her nipples to swell.

"Oh Daniel," Brianna gasped, enjoying his tender touch.

As he delighted in caressing Brianna, a thought occurred to the ghost so he asked, *"How is it that I'm able to touch you without feeling drained?"*

"Water," the witch replied.

"I don't understand," Daniel replied, feeling confused.

"Water has its own form of energy naturally. It's stronger if it's moving, like this creek. Entities, such as yourself and a witch like me, can draw upon this energy. It can soothe you or give you strength. This is why you're able to fondle me without feeling drained."

"I never knew that was possible," Daniel said as he rubbed his hands over Brianna's head, massaging her. *"How long does this last?"*

The witch moaned with enjoyment as she educated the specter, "Depends on you and your use of the excess energy. It will feel great for a while until you use it up, then you'll go back to normal. You can ask for the natural energies from the elementals too. They can provide it as well."

"What are these elementals that you speak of, my sweet Bri?"

"Earth, Air, Fire, Water, and Spirit. Each one has their own unique energy that they can lend you, if you respectfully ask. They can always say no. It's never a good idea to force them to do what you want against their will. Right now, Water elementals are helping me relax and lowering some of my physical pain. Earth is grounding and can restore energy and take any that you don't need. Air is more playful and can make one feel flighty. Fire is full of passion and great for fighting and burning negative things out of the body. Each one can heal or cause you harm. It all depends on how you treat them."

"And Spirit?"

"It's the rarest of the elementals. I haven't interacted with them, but I do make them offerings, along with the other four. It's best to keep them happy and not show too much favoritism to just one or they will be upset and won't work with you. The closest that I've come to dealing with Spirit is with my wolf pack, astral projection, or going on a spirit walk."

"So much that I don't understand. I feel like a fool," Daniel bitterly replied.

"Don't fret over it. I'll tell you everything that I know. You've not been educated on the natural ways of the world. So many people these days aren't. Most don't realize how many strange and wondrous things in nature are all around them."

Cold droplets of rain fell from the cloudy sky, splashing all around them. The ghost removed his hands and stated, *"You need to get out of the water, Bri."*

"It's just a little rain. Nothing to worry about."

Daniel pleaded with the witch, sounding anxious, *"Maybe so, but this creek is treacherous and tends to flood quickly. The shadowy thing has lulled people in here and let them get swept away. I don't want that to happen to you."*

The witch nodded curtly, "You would know this better than me since you've been around here for a long time. Best not to take any chances."

Brianna opened her eyes as she rolled over. She swam back to the bank just as the rain came down in sheets. The witch bent over to grab her sleep shirt and was rewarded with another otherworldly groan of appreciation. Brianna smiled as she turned around, but paused. The ghost was hovering in the creek as it swelled, the current was swifter with plenty of choppy, churning waters.

"Thanks for saving me from my own ignorance, Daniel. When I get dry, I'm going to cleanse and put my protections on the cabin. I hope that you'll be able to come in." Brianna said as she slipped her cotton sleepshirt and her shoes on. Her wet clothes clung snuggly against her body as she briskly walked back to the cabin. The ghost watched the witch as she closed the door to the cabin behind her. He smiled as he hovered in the rushing waters, not because of the influx of power from the creek, but from the fact that for the first time since he died, Daniel felt happiness.

Chuckling caused all of the ghost's joy to erode away. Daniel slowly turned around and saw the shadowy thing on the other side of the creek, malevolently smiling.

"*Do my eyes deceive me or do we have new playthings in our cabin?*" The dark entity asked.

"*You mean my cabin,*" the ghost hissed.

"*When I slaughtered you and your family, the cabin became mine. You couldn't keep it in life so what makes you think you can keep it in death?*" The shadowy thing replied with little remorse.

"*I won't allow you to hurt these people,*" Daniel said as he circled the dark entity. "*I will find a way to end you once and for all!*"

"*Being a tad bit melodramatic aren't we, Daniel? You're like a broken record. Any time someone new lives here, it's the same empty threat. The truth of the matter is that you're all talk and zero action.*"

Daniel growled as he shot towards the shadowy thing, throwing several punches at it. Much to the dark entity's surprise, it felt the blows. The ghost continued its assault, enjoying the extra boost of power from the creek. The shadowy thing managed to block the ghost's next volley of punches.

"Someone seems to have gotten stronger," the shadowy thing stated as it grabbed a hold of the ghost, *"Let's change that right now."*

The dark entity wrapped Daniel in what looked like black frayed ribbons. The specter howled in agony as the otherworldly creature leeched all of his extra power away. The shadowy thing cruelly laughed at the ghost as he attempted to free himself from the bindings but to no avail.

The ghost was barely visible, he faded in and out of existence once the shadowy thing released him. The dark entity got close to Daniel's ear and whispered, *"Let this be a lesson for you, Daniel. No matter what you do. No matter how much power you can obtain, I'll always be the stronger of us both. I would destroy you, but I love having you around as my favorite punching bag."*

"One way...or another..." Daniel replied weakling, *"I'll find...a way... to be...rid of you..."*

"Don't count on it, my old friend," the shadowy thing hissed as it raced towards the

cabin, eagerly wanting to see who his next victims will be. It was about to barge inside, but was repelled. The shadowy thing circled the cabin, trying to find a way in, but failed.

It looked through the window and saw a woman using incense and a bowl of water on everything and on all the entry points. The dark entity snarled as it hit the side of the cabin, *"Fucking little witch! I'll tear your ass apart for this blatant disrespectful behavior!"*

Daniel could only watch on, feeling amused that his personal tormentor was ranting and having difficulty getting inside.

Chapter Nine

Brianna slowly walked around the cabin with a stick of incense and a small bowl filled with blessed water. Her pain was slowly creeping back up but that didn't deter the witch. From what she learned from Daniel; Brianna knew that she needed to put up protections on her new home.

The witch made sure to let the smoke from the incense touch the walls, windows, doors and any other places something could enter. She also made sure to get every nook and cranny so not a single place was missed within the cabin. After using the incense, the witch also dipped her fingers in the bowl of blessed water and flicked it everywhere too.

Brianna always had a pack of incense sticks and blessed water handy for this exact reason. The blessed water was gathered from the Columbia River last summer. She preferred to use a natural source of water because it was stronger than what came out of the sink.

Brianna made it blessed by adding salt to the water, while in a salt circle, and kindly asked any entities of good and positive intent and the elementals to add their protective energies to it. In her mind, this was way better than holy water that one could get from a church.

The reason for this is because it all depends on the priest that puts the blessing on the water and how much of his spiritual intent, he puts into it. If someone is on shaky ground with their faith, then it shows in the strength of the water. By using other entities and her own energy and intent, Brianna had no need for holy water because it was always more potent and powerful.

The witch drew pentagrams on all the doors and windows, using the blessed water, and muttered the mantra, "Nothing negative, harmful, or mischievous may enter or remain. Only those of good and positive intent may enter this space."

By creating this barrier, Brianna could feel if something tries to enter, like a silent alarm in her head. Walking towards the bathroom, the witch felt something probing her work. A feeling of anger and frustration came from whatever it was, along with a few colorful words.

Midnight did his alarm screeched for ten seconds before stating, "*Bad boy outside!*"

Brianna nodded as she walked back in the living room, calmly soothing her bird. When Midnight was calmer, the witch smiled as she called out, "Get used to it. You are *not* allowed in here. Take this as your one and only warning: don't mess with me or those around me."

"*One way or another, witchling,*" the shadowy thing maliciously replied, "*I will find a way in and when I do, you'll wish that you had never been born.*"

"If I had a nickel for every threat that I've heard from entities like yourself," Brianna sarcastically replied as she finished her protections, "I could retire and not have to worry about money ever again."

"*Step outside and let's see who'll be standing last,*" the dark entity replied as it repeatedly hit the front door. The loud bangs caused Brianna to flinch, but her resolve never wavered.

The witch chuckled as she said, "Nah, I'm too tired to deal with you at the moment. How's about you go for a little run and burn off some of that hate."

"*If you think I'm leaving here-*" the shadowy thing's tirade was cut short when it heard the sounds of growling and howls. The dark entity fled as quickly as it could as the pack of spirit wolves gave chase, cursing the entire time. Brianna had an amused smile as she sat down at the dinner table. She could barely make out the silhouette of the ghost as it came inside.

"At least I know that you can come and go as you please," Brianna said as the ghost hovered next to her. She noticed a huge difference in him and she asked, "Are you okay? You don't look so good."

"*I'll manage,*" Daniel half-heartedly laughed, "*The shadowy thing did this to me. It drained me because I attacked it out by the creek.*"

"So *that's* the thing that keeps you here? It's a good thing that I decided to push through the pain and put up my protections then."

"At least you let me in. I don't want to be kicked out of my home," Daniel replied with the hint of a smile. He did enjoy seeing her nude form once again, her wet cotton sleepshirt sat draped over the middle of the sink.

"I had nothing to do with it. It's all on you."

Confused, the ghost asked, *"What are you saying?"*

"If you were here to cause me harm, the barrier wouldn't let you in. I'm sure that you saw how well that worked with your dark buddy. It says a lot about you if you can enter here and I couldn't be any happier."

The ghost stepped behind the witch and ran his hands up and down her shoulders and arm. She shivered but noticed a difference in his touch when compared to earlier out in the creek, "Since my pack is chasing your killer, why not go outside and regain your strength like I showed you."

Daniel looked out the window, his gaze fixed on the flooded creek as he sighed, *"I'm not sure if I can. I feel weak. The shadowy thing has never done that to me before."*

"Are you worried about leaving the cabin," Brianna asked.

"I don't know if I can. It took a lot of effort to get back in here with you, my sweet little Bri."

"Hmm," the witch tapped her index finger on her chin in contemplation, "maybe there's a way to help you from here. Are you open to trying something new?"

"I am. Though, I don't know what can be done. My ignorance is showing once again."

"Good boy, okay?" Midnight asked, sounding worried, *"Good boy, okay please?"*

"Daniel will be well, you little worry wart," Brianna replied as she stood up gingerly. She walked over to the counter in the kitchen and grabbed a container of salt, a bag of graham crackers, and the bowl of blessed water. The witch walked over to the refrigerator and grabbed a bottle of Martinelli's sparkling cider. The witch looked around and decided to use a clear spot in the crowded living room.

She sat the salt container, water bowl, and the food and drink on the floor and scooted a plastic step stool by the items. The witch walked towards the bedroom to gather more of her ritual supplies. Brianna rummaged through a box that was labeled 'altar' and picked up a small cast iron cauldron, a package of incense sticks and a wooden holder, a box of matches, a red candle, a goddess statue, and a small smooth rock.

When Brianna stepped out of her bedroom, the conure saw what she had in her hands and got excited. The bird climbed on the bars of the cage and repeatedly yanked on the locked latch.

"I know, baby," Brianna smiled at her familiar, "You know what momma is fixing to do?"

"*Yeah! Help momma!*" Midnight yelled loudly.

The witch sat her supplies down on a small plastic step stool. She pulled out the wooden holder and inserted an incense stick in a small hole in it. Next to it, Brianna sat the bowl of blessed water next to the cast iron cauldron. She placed the red candle and the smooth rock together.

"Is there any significance where you place those things," Daniel curiously asked.

"Yes, normally, but because those that I work with are my friends, they will overlook my lapses in remembering proper placement. Intent matters more than anything," Brianna replied as she set the goddess statue behind the cast iron cauldron, "but I do prefer my statue representation of Gaia is right here."

"What's Gaia?"

"Gaia is Mother Earth. She is also my patron goddess. The one that I gave oaths to long ago. I pledged my life to protect the weak and the innocent. I'm a warrior for her and will fight all my battles in Her name. In turn, She aids me with knowledge, strength, and even Her presence when She feels that I need it. My path is a hard solitary road, but what journey isn't?"

"But from what I've observed," the ghost said as the witch opened the spout on the salt

container and slowly poured it on the floor, *"you don't travel it alone."*

"You're right. A Warrior of Gaia is never truly alone, otherworldly speaking. Jess doesn't believe in the supernatural, even though he's sensitive to energy. I try to do my craft when he's not around so I don't have to listen to his snide comments."

Brianna left a small gap in the salt circle. She stood up and walked over to Midnight's cage. She leaned down and purred, "You know that momma's about to do some magic?"

The conure let out a high-pitched chirp. Brianna smiled lovingly as she asked, "Do you want to help me in the circle?"

"Yeah!" Midnight replied with excitement as he curled and rapidly bobbed his head happily. The witch took the clip off the cage door lever and immediately, the bird yanked it open. He excitedly chattered as he flew out of his cage and landed in the middle of the salt circle.

The witch walked back into the bedroom and grabbed a long shirt. She slipped it on as she softly groaned, her pain increased with each passing second. Brianna knew that she should rest and take it easy, but she couldn't allow Daniel to stay in her home in his current condition. She wanted to show her appreciation for the ghost's warning, it was the least the witch could do. Brianna hoped that what she had in mind would work.

Chapter Ten

The witch slowly made her way to the salt circle, grimacing slightly as she sat down on the floor. Daniel looked at her, wishing that this woman wouldn't fuss with her craft because of what happened to him. He knew that no good would come from protesting, the specter could see her stubborn conviction and he discovered that it made him love her even more.

"Get in the circle with me, please," Brianna said with her eyes closed. The conure grabbed a beak full of the witch's shirt and slowly climbed up to perch on her shoulder. The ghost shimmered in and out of existence as he made his way into the ritual circle. Daniel felt a tidal wave of uncertainty and concern. His religious mindset was screaming hellfire and damnation and yet, with Brianna doing this ritual, Daniel felt oddly at peace.

Brianna grabbed the salt container and said, "Okay, I'm going to close and charge the circle and ground myself. When I do this, you can't leave the circle. This is a safe space for any entities that decide to join us. It's also to protect us from any that wish us harm. So, whatever you do, *don't* break the circle."

"I'll do my best. Other than that, what do you want me to do?"

"Nothing. Just stay there and be prepared for it to get crowded in here. You never know who or what will show up."

As the ghost nodded, Brianna poured the salt, filling in the gap in the circle. She set the salt container to the side and slowly breathed with her eyes closed as she got in a meditative state. Daniel could see her entire body relaxing, her breathing came in at a slow, rhythmic pace. The ghost could see energy flow through the salt like a flame eating away at a trail of gunpowder. The specter also saw what appeared to be roots coming from Brianna's heart shaped ass. The roots burrowed quietly through the floor, easily pushing through the soil under the cabin.

The witch opened her eyes as she picked up the box of matches. The specter intently observed as Brianna pulled out a match and ignited it, using the side of the box. The witch held the flickering flame against the wick of the candle and said, "Elements of Fire, I asked that you join our circle, please."

The candle flame flickered and danced, which the witch said, "Thank you."

Brianna tossed the burning match into the cauldron to extinguish itself. She picked up the incense stick and put the tip in the candle flame. Once the tip was burning, the witch blew on it to ensure that it stayed lit. With the smoke wisping in the air, Brianna said, "Elements of Air, we ask that you join our circle, please."

A breeze playfully with strands of the witch's hair, which made her smile. Brianna glanced down at the bowl of water and said, "Elements of Water, we ask that you join our circle, please." A cool sensation cascaded over her body like a liquid embrace. Brianna shifted slightly, the roots that she used to ground herself to the Earth made it difficult to move much.

"Elements of Earth, we ask that you join our circle, please," the witch asked. Brianna felt a warm embrace, like her body was nestled in a protective cocoon. Daniel couldn't believe what he was witnessing. He could actually see the elementals at times.

The witch called out once more, "All those of good and positive intent, please join our circle." She glanced over at Daniel and added, "Now, it will be getting crowded in here."

More entities stepped into the salt circle; many the ghost didn't recognize. Several beings were tall, pale and had pointy ears. They wore bright and colorful clothing and had long hair. Silverwolf stepped in next, looking irritated.

Daniel was startled by the sight of an enormous reptilian head that was covered in scales and spikes. Its mouth was lined with deadly looking teeth. The creature was in the circle but not fully here, which made the specter wonder how big it was. Pint size people flew around, their wings fluttered like a dragonfly does and looked similar to each other.

Brianna spoke once again, "Gaia and any other deities of good and positive intent, I ask that you join us in our circle, please."

As they waited, Silverwolf spoke with disgust, "The hunt continues. The creature managed to jump through multiple dimensions to the point where we couldn't follow."

"You did your best, Silver," the witch replied solemnly, "You and the pack will get another chance at it. It was stupid enough to threaten me."

"Why are you doing this?" The spirit alpha wolf asked, "I can see that you're not well. You know better than this."

"Daniel is the reason. He needs our help."

"We scared the threat off," Silver snarled at the ghost, "You can leave now."

"*If only it...were that simple. The shadowy thing...keeps me tied...to this place.*" Daniel replied, feeling lethargic as he shimmered in and out of existence. His voice sounded like it was taking a great deal of effort to speak.

"What are you going to do about it?" A strong and commanding voice spoke as a curvy woman appeared in front of the witch. She looked down at Brianna with a calm, emotionless face as she added, "If there's to be a fight, I suggest you take care of it and then go rest."

"Welcome Gaia," Brianna replied. She pointed at the ghost and said, "I'm casting this circle in the hopes that any of you could give him some healing energy."

"*Midnight help good boy!*" The conure chirped up as he looked at Daniel.

"You're putting yourself through this torture for a damn *ghost*?" Silverwolf growled as he eyed the specter.

"*Help momma!*" Midnight replied as he puffed up, swaying side to side.

"*Is this necessary...I'm sure that... I'll be fine...*"

"He's a victim in several ways, Silver," the witch said as she defiantly crossed her arms across chest, "Daniel is under my protection. If you don't like it, you can leave."

"If this ghost needs healing," one of the tall pale entities spoke calmly, "then he should be the one to ask for it."

"Brianna, you know that we are always willing to help those in need, but only if they ask for it," the other tall pale entity added with a knowing look.

The witch rolled her eyes as she looked at Daniel. The ghost looked back at her and asked, *"What are they...referring to, Bri?"*

"These fae are pointing out that I should do the same. Healing energy takes hold better if one asks for it and consent is given," Brianna replied as she stuck her tongue out at the fae beings.

"So, why not... ask for yourself…," the ghost looked her over and could tell that the witch needed it, *"I hate seeing... you in...so much pain…my sweet Bri..."*

The witch shrugged her shoulders, "Your needs are greater than mine at the moment. Just ask for assistance, please."

Daniel thought for a moment and then replied, *"I shall...if you...agree to... do it...with me..."*

Brianna groaned loudly in frustration, "Fine, but you go first."

All eyes fell on the ghost. At this moment, Daniel wanted nothing more than to flee from their scrutinizing collective gazes. He gulped as he spoke, *"Please...grant me...your...healing energy..."*

One by one, the different entities within the circle took turns placing their hands on the specter, with the exception of Silverwolf. Daniel closed his eyes, feeling a significant difference in the way he felt. Brianna smiled as she watched the ghost become more stabilized.

Daniel opened his eyes and lovingly looked down at the witch. Midnight chirped up, *"Pretty boy! No ow now!"*

The specter motioned to Brianna and said, *"Your turn, my sweet Bri."*

The witch blushed slightly as she stuck her tongue out at the ghost, "Fine, but only because we made a promise to you. All of those of good and positive intent, I ask that you give me your healing energy, please."

One by one, the different entities within the circle took turns placing their hands on the witch, even Silverwolf. Daniel wondered if the spirit wolf didn't easily trust others. Brianna's lips parted slightly with each wave of magic entered her body. Her breathing was slow and deep. The conure bobbed his head happily as he chirped up, *"Momma no ow! Momma okay!"*

When everyone finished, Brianna meekly said, "Thank you."

"Do you have a plan to rid this area of the dark creature roaming the area," Silver asked, his voice etched with both concern and determination.

"Not at the moment," the witch replied, sounding exhausted to the ghost, "I'm still recovering from not only the move, but all the stress from the last month."

"I still believe that me and the pack should shred Jess until there's nothing identifiable left of him," the spirit alpha wolf growled, glaring all around as if he was looking for the witch's boyfriend. The other entities were murmuring in agreement.

"And then I wouldn't be able to afford this place," Brianna irritably answered, "If I can get my website design business to bring in steady income, I'd send him packing to go live with his mother."

"There are ways around her relationship issues," Gaia spoke up, which caused everyone to go silent. The goddess put a hand on Brianna's shoulder and used her other hand to pet Midnight. The bird croaked happily as the goddess spoke, "What is the situation with the dark creature?"

"I only know of what Daniel said to me earlier. It killed him and his entire family, but keeps him stuck here to torture him. I'm grateful for his warning, which is why I put my protections up on my new home. If not, it could have been a different story." Brianna replied as she looked at the goddess, knowing full well what was coming.

"Then you know what you *must* do," Gaia calmly ordered, "Gather your strength and prepare to deal with this threat. Call on what allies you need."

"I shall do it," the witch replied but then she had a confused look as she asked, "What exactly did you mean by there are ways around the relationship?"

Gaia briefly glanced at Daniel before cryptically saying, "Fight and we shall see what happens next."

Chapter Eleven

The witch nodded as she thanked everyone for attending her circle. One by one, the different entities exited the ritual as Brianna uncharged the salt. She ran a finger through the salt circle, breaking the barrier. The witch grabbed one of the graham crackers and took a bite. Next, the witch took a sip of the sparkling cider and shared both with Midnight and then she stood up.

Brianna gathered the food and drink and slowly walked over to the front door, after leaving Midnight on her desk chair. When she opened the door, Daniel hovered next to her, feeling confused, and asked, *"What are you doing, Bri? It's pouring rain out."*

"You see these?" The witch asked. Daniel nodded so Brianna continued, "These are my offerings that I'm giving as a way of saying thanks for attending my circle. I don't have to leave the porch, so stop worrying."

The ghost nodded as he observed the witch. She poured the contents of the glass on the saturated ground and said, "For those that attended my circle, I offer this sparkling cider to quench your thirst."

Brianna crumbled up the graham crackers and sprinkled them on the ground while saying, "For those that attended my circle, I offer these graham crackers as a way of saying thanks."

The witch hobbled back inside the cabin. She walked over to a wall of boxes and grabbed a small Shop-Vac. As Brianna vacuumed up the salt, the ghost admonished, *"You should go rest. I can tell that you need it. Why must you clean this up now?"*

The witch sighed as her weary shoulders sagged, "Jess will throw a fit if I don't. He doesn't like it when I cast circles or do anything pagan. So, if I don't get it cleaned up, there will be another argument tonight. It's not worth it."

"I see," Daniel replied as he watched her shut off the vacuum and pushed it against the wall. Brianna walked over and slowly gathered her ritual items as the ghost lamented, *"I wish that I could be of service to you.*

I would gladly clean this up for you, my sweet little Bri."

As the witch walked into the bedroom, she sadly replied, "Everyone says that to me."

Daniel hovered in her peripheral vision and said, *"But I truly mean what I say."*

Brianna found a semi-empty box and set her craft items in it, grimacing as she said, "I know that you do. You're dead and can't physically interact with corporeal things. You have a good reason right there. I'm just used to everyone saying it when in reality, none would stick around for long."

"Because of Jess?" Daniel asked.

"Yes, but also all of my health issues," Brianna said as she walked out of the bedroom, "Sure guys say that they want to take care of me, but as soon as my medical issues become too much of a burden, they find a reason to leave me. Quite frankly, I don't blame them."

As Brianna finished vacuuming and put the Shop-Vac away, the conure flew to her shoulder, so she walked over to his cage. She put her shoulder against the cage, Midnight climbed off and into it. The bird got inside and immediately turned around for kisses. The witch smiled lovingly at her familiar as he demanded, "*Momma night night right now!*"

"Do you want to go night night, Midnight?"

"*No,*" the conure reiterated, pleading with the witch to listen, "*Momma!*"

"Oh, you want *me* to go lay down?"

Midnight chattered happily as he bobbed his head vigorously. Brianna latched the cage door shut and placed a small clip on it to lock it. She shuffled back into the bedroom where the specter patiently waited for her. Brianna was exhausted and the old spring mattress bed was beckoning to her as she took her clothes off.

As she crawled in, the witch murmured when she noticed the ghost leaving, "Don't go. Stay with me, Daniel."

Daniel paused and then turned to face her, "*Are you sure? I don't want to disturb your respite time.*"

"I love your presence. I can't explain why, but I do."

The ghost came near the bed and hesitantly asked, *"Will the lady of the house permit me to lie down with her?"*

"Please do. I trust you Daniel," Brianna answered with no hesitancy and then added with a mischievous grin, "Hmmm."

"What's on my favorite witch's cunning mind?"

"I'm going to meditate and do a spirit walk. Would you care to join me?"

"Sure, though I'm not sure what to do, my dear," the ghost answered.

"Just listen to my words and focus on me and we can have a little bit of fun together."

The specter nodded as he intently listened to Brianna's words, his eyes fixated on her rhythmic moving breasts. The witch closed her eyes and said calmly, "Imagine being in a large meadow. Little flowers and tall grass swaying with the wind. There's not a cloud in the sky as the sun kisses our bare skin."

Daniel felt enthralled by the witch's colorful descriptions that he didn't realize that he was now standing in the meadow. A large sprawling forest stood sentinel at the edge of the tranquil meadow, Daniel could see Brianna stepping into the tree line, beckoning him to join her.

The ghost moved effortlessly towards her; his excitement showed as he swiftly followed. The light from the sun grew dimmer as the thick canopy absorbed it. Daniel trailed behind the witch, wondering where exactly she was taking him.

The sound of slow trickling water grew as he neared a stream. Brianna waded into the middle of it, motioning with her index finger for him to follow. Daniel could see that the witch had nothing on, except for a flirty, mischievous grin.

As he approached, the ghost reached out instinctively and managed to caress Brianna on her soft cheek. Daniel gasped as she giggled, "How is this possible, witch?"

"We're in the spirit realm," Brianna explained as she walked slowly around him, letting her hand run over his ethereal body, "I come here to transform into my spirit animal and go for a run with the other spirit wolves. Here, we can touch each other. Does that please you, Daniel?"

The ghost ran a hand over his mouth as he groaned with pleasure. Brianna looked like an angel sent from Heaven, just for him, as the water from the stream lapped against her naked form. The witch wrapped her arms around the ghost, causing him to stiffen from contact.

Daniel relaxed as Brianna kissed the back of his neck, steering her wet lips up to his ear. The ghost didn't understand completely how this was possible, but he wasn't going to pass up a chance to love on this woman. It had been over a hundred years since he had been intimate with a woman.

Daniel spun around and pressed his ethereal lips against hers, fearing that he may not get another chance. Brianna groaned as her hands wandered up and down the ghost's body as he tightened his embrace. The witch could feel his member stirring as their bodies were pressed against each other, which made her giggle as she asked, "So, how long has it been since someone took ahold of your plow, farmer?"

"*Too long, my sweet little Bri,*" Daniel sheepishly replied, "*Hopefully, I can remember how to use it.*"

Brianna smiled as she slipped her hand down into the ghost's pants, stroking his rock-hard member, "I'm confident that you will know what to do with this, Daniel. Care to plow my field?"

Daniel groaned, barely registering her remark as he felt his pants getting tugged down. He lifted the witch up in his arms, taking her by surprise, and managed to walk back to the bank as his pants trickled down to his ankles.

The ghost smiled lovingly at Brianna as he set her down, maneuvering his pelvis between her thighs. He leaned forward and kissed her lips as he snaked a finger inside the witch's slick core while using his thumb to stimulate her clit, causing her to gasp.

"Oh, Daniel," Brianna moaned, "Gods that feels so good."

The ghost chuckled next to her ear as he slipped another finger inside her, *"I don't think that I'll ever get used to hearing you say my name like that. I want to hear you moan it even more."*

Brianna hungrily eyed Daniel as he pressed his lips on each of her breasts, licking and nibbling on her nipples. She grabbed handfuls of his hair as the ghost increased the speed of his finger thrusts. Their eyes locked on each other as she begged, "Please Daniel. I want you inside me!"

"Are you sure? I do enjoy seeing you squirm under my touch."

The witch playfully growled, "Fuck me now or so help me I'll white light you!"

The ghost shifted to his knees, holding his member at the witch's slick core, *"Someone's a little impatient tonight. Are you sure that you truly want this? Do you want me?"*

Brianna chewed on her quivering bottom lip, "It's been a long time since I've had...something hard inside me. Other than one of my many toys."

Daniel incredulously bit out, "*Seriously? That boy won't even be intimate with you either?*"

"Jess has trouble getting it up, if you know what I mean. His diet is poor and his diabetes causes him to be more of a hold up than a stick up, if you catch my meaning. He never lasts more than a few minutes before going limp."

"*Hmm,*" the ghost mused, "*I'm not familiar with diabetes, but I know that you deserve someone that can bring you pleasure for a longer duration. I'll see if I can fill the void, my sweet little Bri.*"

Daniel pushed his member inside her, causing the witch to gasp. He slowly but gently pressed further inside Brianna, not wanting to hurt her. The ghost was caught by surprise when she wrapped her legs around his waist, urging him on, "Fuck me, Daniel! I want you *now*!"

"*As you wish, my love,*" Daniel grinned as he pushed the full length of his member deep inside her, causing her to moan. Brianna dug her heels into the ghost's ass as she tried to match his thrusts. As Daniel increased his speed, a strange buzzing sound caught his attention. He looked around, expecting to see a swarm of bees nearby, but all he saw was the forest and the creek.

Brianna breathlessly asked, "What's wrong...Daniel?"

"I hear a strange buzzing sound. Almost like there's a hive of bees right on top of us, yet I see none."

The witch thought for a moment and then she giggled, causing the ghost to look at, feeling confused. Brianna replied as she heavily panted, "That's...my vibrator...that you're...hearing..."

"Am I not adequate enough for you?" The ghost paused.

"You are, Daniel," Brianna said as she stroked his cheek lovingly, "Spiritually, this feels wonderful, but in the physical world, I need to do this to properly get off. If not, our love making will feel like a long teasing session, which can cause my body to become tense and lead to more pain. It has nothing to do with what you're doing. I just wish we could fuck physically. You're not mad at me, are you?"

Daniel replied without hesitation, *"No. I don't believe that I could ever be mad at you. I'd also feel guilty if I caused you an ounce of discomfort. This is something that I need to get used to, if you'll have me here again."*

Brianna smiled as she hummed a song. The ghost couldn't quite place it, but as the witch bursted out in a giggle fit, he asked, *"What song is that that's making you so jovial?"*

"My version of the song of "*The Birds and the Bees*". I've changed a few lyrics to say *'It's the ghost and the bees, my pussy's dripping between his knees.'*"

The ghost wasn't sure what to make of this strange ditty, but as long as it made Brianna happy, he didn't care. He leaned down and kissed her lips as she said, "I definitely want to do this with you again, but we need to get back. As much fun as this is, I need some good sleep, Daniel."

The ghost nodded as he found himself next to the witch. He watched as she rolled over onto her stomach with the vibrator still on and somewhat inside her core.

"Good night, Daniel," Brianna murmured with her eyes closed.

Daniel laid next to the witch like a lover would do. The witch smiled as a slight shiver ran through her body as he pressed his ethereal lips on the back of her neck, *"Rest well, my sweet little Bri."*

Chapter Twelve

Several weeks had passed. The witch and the ghost kept playing around in the spirit world, much to Daniel's delight. Brianna sent out a portfolio of the different website designs she created to several big companies in the hopes that she could do more freelance work and get more clients to work with.

Jess still had his IT job, but was still complaining about the pay. Brianna kept encouraging him to go to work and keep an eye out for a better paying employer, but she could already see signs that her boyfriend was planning on losing this job.

Every time he was getting ready to leave, Jess would whine about how boring the night shift was, watching printers print and documenting any errors that occur. He complained about his manager coming to him and telling him what to do, which was the different assignments needed for the shift.

Tonight, Jess was buzzed and engrossed in WoW, with a box of pizza, a bag of chips, a six pack of beer, and multiple bottles of Mountain Dew covering his desk space. He took his headset, grabbed his phone and immediately Brianna knew what was coming.

"Just go to work, Jess," the witch pleaded with her hands firmly on her hips, "It's too soon to call in sick. Can't you just wait until you get past your ninety-day probation?"

Jess ignored her as he called the manager on duty, trying to sound miserable over the phone, "Hello, Steve? This is Jess. I'm sorry to say that I'm not feeling well and won't be able to come in tonight."

"That's unfortunate. We're already down a couple of people. Are you sure that you can't make it?"

"Yeah, I'm sure," Jess dramatically coughed and wheezed, "I have a high fever and a bad cough. I don't want to get any of the other employees sick."

Begrudgingly, Steve replied, *"Understandable. Get better soon. We need you, Jess."* His manager ended the call before he could say another word. Jess smiled and shrugged his shoulders as he tossed the phone on the desk. He opened a beer and took a swig from it as Brianna got in his face, "Why must you do this?"

"Do what," he replied with an alcohol laced belch.

The witch crinkled her nose in disgust, "Choose gaming over having a roof over our heads."

"I work hard so I deserve a little me time every once in a while. Besides, your website design gigs can cover it, especially if you get hired for one of those companies you applied to the other day. It would be nice to see you pull your weight financially around here," Jess stated matter of fact.

Brianna fumed angrily as she reached behind Jess's desk while he was chatting with his Wow buddies over his headset and yanked the power cord out from the tower. Jess growled as he tossed his headset off, "Why the hell did you do that? I was in the middle of a dungeon run."

"If you're so sick," Brianna huffed in frustration, "then maybe you should go lay down and rest."

Jess quickly stood up, knocking his swivel chair over in the process. He grabbed Brianna roughly by her arm and forcefully dragged her towards the bedroom.

"Let go," the witch cried out, "You're hurting me!"

"You've been getting pretty snippety with me lately and quite frankly, I'm sick of your attitude, Bri. It's high time that you learn your place!"

"*Bad daddy!*" Midnight screeched, trying with all his might to open his locked cage door but to no avail, "*No ow my momma!*"

"Piss off, Midnight or you're next!" Jess retorted.

As they got in the bedroom, Jess pinned the witch face down on the foot of the bed. He managed to hold both of her arms behind her back as she kicked and squirmed. Jess snatched up a piece of nylon rope off the floor and roughly tied her wrists together.

"Let me go, you asshole!" Brianna screamed as Jess pressed his hand on her back, keeping her in place. She heard a metallic rattling noise coming from behind her, but couldn't turn her head enough to see what it was.

"I don't think so, *sweetheart*," Jess coldly remarked next to her ear, the smell of alcohol and stale food assailing her nostrils. He sat a leather belt in front of her face, causing Brianna to flinch, and added, "I think that it's high time that I beat that sass out of you."

"You do this, you better sleep with one eye open," the witch threatened, but could only watch as he picked the belt up.

"I'm the man of this shit hole and you *will* respect me, *babe*," Jess replied as he swung the belt, it smacked firmly on Brianna's ass.

"You're barely passable for a man-OUCH! Stop it!"

Jess seemed to grow angrier with each strike, causing a lot of long red welts to appear. The witch cried but concentrated on her breathing, trying to block out the pain. Brianna yelped loudly with each blow, which caught the ghost's attention as he entered the cabin.

He flew into the bedroom and was shocked at what he saw happening. Daniel instantly saw red as he watched his helpless witch being incapacitated, crying as her boyfriend beat on her. The ghost roared, which caused Brianna to wonder where the sound came from, as he flew directly at Jess. He wanted to knock this man into a wall and, hopefully, break his neck.

"Bitch, you *will* fucking obey- Ahhh!"

Daniel wasn't sure what was going on when he made contact with Jess, but something was amiss. Brianna felt a shift on the bed as her boyfriend's hand let go of her. She saw Jess lying next to her convulsing like he was having a seizure. Brianna dropped down to her knees, watching him thrashing around violently.

Brianna tugged and pulled on her bindings, but they didn't budge so she decided to crawl on her knees and into the kitchen to find a knife. She grunted painfully as her knees made contact with each grueling step. The conure watched on helplessly as the witch made it to the sink.

"Let me out! Help momma, please!" Midnight demanded with a hint of sorrow.

"I wish that I could, baby. Momma can't even stand up at the moment or I would."

The sound of something hitting the floor caught the witch's attention. She wondered if Jess fell off the bed while he was seizing or if he was stumbling around in the bedroom. Frantically, Brianna looked for a knife, but there was none in reach. She wanted to be free from her bindings and also have a weapon in case Jess came after her again.

She tried to use her chin on the edge of the counter top to lift herself up, but her legs weren't strong enough to support her. Another crash caught her attention as she saw Jess sprawled out on the floor by the bedroom doorway, muttering profanities to himself.

"Stay back, asshole!" Brianna yelled at him, "You come any closer to me and I'll bite your limp biscuit off!"

"I'm sorry, my sweet little Bri," Jess replied, looking haggard and his voice changed, "I'm not sure what's going on at the moment. I can't move well."

"You tied me up and beat me with a belt. I swear, when I'm free, I'll return the favor with my cast iron skillet, Jess!"

Confused, Jess looked at Brianna as he attempted to stand up, his legs were wobbly, "If I can get the hang of this body, I'll untie you. I'm not Jess."

"You're right," the witch sneered in disgust, "I don't know who you are anymore."

"*Good boy,*" Midnight chirped up, "*Help momma please?*"

"I'm trying, Midnight. It feels so strange being able to feel things, let alone breathe air once again."

Brianna eyed her boyfriend and noticed a few subtle changes. His face seemed distorted, like another face was at war with his normal visage. His voice was different, but sounded familiar, and didn't sound like Jess at all. She wondered if his seizure was the cause for this change, but then she recalled what the conure said to her boyfriend.

"Is that daddy, Midnight?"

The conure eyed Jess for a moment and then said, "*No. Good boy now. No ow momma.*"

"I would *never* hurt my sweet little Bri. You deserve a real man and not that cowardly worm you're living with," Jess replied calmly.

At that moment, it dawned on the witch what she was seeing, "Daniel? Is that you in there?"

"Yes," the ghost said as he gazed at his hands, looking confused at what he was witnessing, "but I'm not sure what happened. I saw Jess hurting you so I tried to knock him down. I'm so confused. What did I do?"

"You *jumped* him," Brianna replied with surprise.

"What?" Daniel blurted out.

"You jumped him. Think of it as a form of possession, kind of like what demons do, except you're a ghost. Similar principle. Now if you can manage to free me, I'd be grateful."

Daniel nodded as he attempted to work Jess's body. His movements reminded the witch of a marionette with a terrible puppeteer, all wobbly and out of sync with his normal fluid gait. Daniel gave Brianna a wry smile and said, "Give me a moment. It's been a long time since I've inhabited a physical body."

When he got to the witch, Daniel reached out for her and she flinched. She looked up at his confused visage and sadly said, "Sorry. I didn't mean to do that."

"I suppose that is to be expected. This is the body of the one that just hurt you," he looked at the front door and added, "If you want, just say the word and I'll gladly walk him into the creek and he'll never hurt you again."

Brianna's lips parted slightly, but then she said, "No, he's not worth it. Just untie me and help me up."

"Right. Help you first and murder your boyfriend later. Got it," Daniel smirked as he worked his fingers to loosen the rope. He grumbled with frustration; Jess's fingers weren't wanting to cooperate.

"Take your time," Brianna said as she grimaced, "Like you said, it's been a while since you've been in a human body."

Daniel took a deep breath and focused on the knot. Before long, the rope became slack and Brianna was able to wiggle her wrists free. She looked at the possessed body of her boyfriend and gave him a long hug, tears streaming down her cheeks.

"There there, my sweet little Bri," Daniel gently rubbed her back, "You're safe with me. Let's get you to the bedroom so I can examine the damage *he* caused."

The witch nodded as he assisted her to her feet. They slowly walked back towards the bedroom, each supporting one another as the conure made kissing sounds.

"Momma is okay. I'm going to go lay down," Brianna said as they stopped by his cage. She leaned in and let Midnight kiss her perched lips repeatedly. It seemed to calm him down enough for the witch to cover him up for the night. As the couple walked into the bedroom, the shadowy thing hovered near a window, grumbling angrily, "*Pathetic boy.*

Can't even get the girl to come outside. Though Daniel has given me a splendid idea on how to get to the witch. Both of them, like Daniel, will be mine!"

Midnight, despite being covered up, turned and looked at the window. He puffed up and yelled with enough magical intent to cause the dark entity to flinch like it had been slapped, "*MY MOMMA! BACK OFF, BAD BOY!"*

Chapter Thirteen

Brianna looked down at the base of her bed and saw Jess's belt. Blood had stained the wooden floor where it sat as a confirmation of what took place here not that long ago. Daniel escorted her to her side of the bed and turned the blanket back for her. She cringed as she laid down on her stomach, "How bad is it?"

"The skin is torn in several spots and there's bruising forming where the welts are." Daniel said as he closely inspected her ass. The witch pointed over at a shelf by the window and said, "Could I sweet talk you into rubbing some Aloe lotion on it?"

"Which one is it?"

"It's a clear bottle with the green goo in it and a yellow lid. You can't miss it."

Daniel nodded as he walked over and grabbed the bottle. He looked it over as he slowly made his way to the bed. Brianna said as he sat down beside her, "It's good for sunburns or burns in general, but it's good for wound care because it helps speed up the healing process. There's a little spigot on the lid that you can squirt it out of so you don't need to take the cap off."

Daniel looked at her, a sympathetic gaze crossed his visage, "I apologize in advance. I'm sure that this will hurt."

The witch sighed, "Unfortunately, I'm used to pain. Just rub it in and then blow on it so it will take some of the burning sensation away."

Brianna braced herself by taking several deep breaths, bracing for contact. Daniel wasn't sure how much to use so he flipped the spigot open and squeezed a decent amount in his hand. He sniffed the strange goo as he coated his palm in it. He placed his hand on the worst area on Brianna's ass, causing her to flinch and gasp.

Daniel glanced at her, worried etched into his eyes, but the witch assured him, "Don't worry, just rub it in, Daniel. It needs to be done."

He got up and straddled her leg, using both of his hands to massage the gel in. Brianna smiled as she relaxed but every so often, she would flinch. Daniel leaned down and slowly blew on her ass, causing little goosebumps to spring up and her to shiver. As the Aloe dried completely, the witch looked over her shoulder and said, "Thank you. That really helped."

Daniel sheepishly grinned, "I'm glad to hear that. Does any other part of your body need my attention?"

The witch nibbled on her bottom lip, unsure how to respond. Daniel could see the war of emotions in her eyes and facial expressions so he added, "I know that you see the *boy* that just abused you so I can understand your reluctance. I'll not pressure you into doing anything that you don't want to do."

Even through his jeans, Brianna could feel his member pressing against her thighs, something that Jess hadn't accomplished in a while. The only way that she found to keep his erection hard for more than a few minutes was by using a cock ring. Daniel seemed to not need one being in her boyfriend's body.

"I appreciate your kind words, but right now I want to experience you fully. I'm not sure how long you can stay in Jess's body, but I for one want to take full advantage of it. Can you feel him? Is he awake?"

Daniel closed his eyes as he removed his shirt and said, "Yes, I feel him. It appears that he's in the background, snoring."

"Must've been the alcohol that made him more prone to possession," the witch replied as she felt Daniel roll off of her and stand next to the bed. She turned on her side, admiring him as he unbuttoned his jeans and let them slide down to his ankles. Brianna noticed the different, yet subtle, changes to Jess's body. Areas seemed toned, muscular curvatures that normally flabby or nonexistent.

Daniel tugged off his boxers and the witch's eyes bulged. She licked her lips as she thought, *"Damn, he's even bigger down there too!"*

The witch motioned with her finger, beckoning him, "Come here, my love. Let me show my appreciation for your help."

Daniel grinned as slowly walked towards her, swaying his hips so his member would bounce a little. Brianna greedily reached out and pulled him onto the bed and kissed Daniel on the lips. Daniel ran his hands up and down the witch's back, trying to be careful not to touch her wounded ass. He kissed his way from her lips and slowly made his way to the witch's neck, causing her to moan.

Brianna turned her head so that he could have better access to her neck as she clawed his back. Despite being in Jess's body, she noticed that Daniel made his body smell different somehow. He had an earthy odor, like freshly tilled soil and cedar, and Brianna loved it and found it intoxicating.

Daniel eyed her possessively as he kissed his way down past her neck, softly letting his lips caress her collar bone. Brianna grabbed handfuls of his hair as she squirmed underneath him, feeling his hard member grinding against her core.

"Do you like that?" Daniel playfully asked.

Brianna growled, "What do you think? Are you going to take me or not?"

Daniel smirked as he kissed his way down to the witch's ample breasts and suckled on each one. He reached his hand down and slowly rubbed Brianna's clit with his thumb while massaging her slick core, causing her to gasp.

"Eventually, I will, my sweet little Bri," Daniel said and then went back to teasing her nipples with his tongue, occasionally blowing on them. "So, tell me, how long has it been since you've been with a real man?"

"Too long," Brianna whimpered as she moaned, "Don't make me beg. I want you inside me!"

"Inside here?" Daniel replied mischievously as he slipped a finger into her wet core.

"Yes! Oh, fuck yes!"

He pushed his finger deeper inside the witch slowly, still playing with her swollen clit with his thumb. Brianna moaned as her core clinched around his finger. The witch bucked her hips as she locked her pleading eyes with him, "Daniel, take me!"

Daniel smirked as he pressed lips against hers, "Sure thing, my sweet little Bri. Why the rush? Don't you want to savor this moment?"

The witch nervously bit her bottom lip and replied with a shaky voice, "Of course I do. It's just that, well, I'm not sure how long you can stay in his body. It takes a lot of energy and effort to do that, especially if you're not inside him willingly."

He nodded, understanding what she was conveying. The ghost was feeling a little fatigued, but he thought that it was from all the physical enjoyment he was having with Brianna.

I'll not allow her to go unsatisfied. Definitely won't let this boy take back control until I'm done.

Daniel leaned back on his knees and edged the tip of his member at her opening. He slowly pushed his 'volunteered' member into the witch, causing her to gasp. Daniel put her legs on his shoulders as he pushed deeper into her core, increasing his thrusts.

"Oh gods," Brianna bit out, "Mmmm, that's it!"

Daniel's eyes rolled back, his eyes fluttering at the sensation of having sex. He grinned wildly as he fucked Brianna as if it might be the last time. For all the ghost knew, it might be.

"Are you enjoying this as much as I am, my love," Daniel asked, panting hard from exertion.

Brianna rocked her pelvis, matching his thrusts, "Gods yes!"

Daniel felt like he was addicted to the witch, each spasm in her core was milking his member, which spurred him to go faster.

"Daniel..." Brianna panted breathlessly, "I'm coming... like I've... never have... before..."

The witch could feel Daniel's member getting bigger and pulsating. She took her legs off his shoulders and wrapped them around his sweaty hips, digging her heels into his ass. She could feel his orgasm building and, for the first time in her life, Brianna felt an orgasm brewing deep inside.

Brianna's cheeks were flush as she grabbed handfuls of his hair and moaned, "Come... for me...my love...Gods... I'm going... to explode..."

Daniel looked at her and replied through gritted teeth, "I don't think... that will be...a hard request... to fill..."

The ghost cried out as his semen came out in quick spurts. Brianna screamed as her eyes fluttered, feeling her own orgasmic bliss kicking in as soon as his hot seed poured deep inside her slick core. Daniel could feel the contractions in her core as his witch's little body greedily milked every bit of semen from him.

Daniel pulled out of her and collapsed beside his witch, heavily breathing with a grin. He looked over at Brianna, caressing her sweaty cheek lovingly, "That was...like nothing that...I've ever experienced...in my life..."

Brianna grinned back at him and said, "Well, when you go witch, you'll *never* switch." Her smile faded as she could see the ghost shifting in Jess's body, knowing that he wouldn't be in there for much longer. She rolled over to her bedside table and pulled out two pairs of handcuffs and a lengthy chain. Daniel wasn't sure what she was going to, but she ordered, "Lay on your stomach, Daniel. There's something that I need to do before you leave me."

The ghost complied and said, "I'll never leave you, my sweet little Bri. What's this for?"

"Hands behind your back and put your feet together, my love," the witch said, a dark shadow crossed her visage, "I need to do this so I can have a little chat with Jess."

Daniel curtly nodded as she snapped the handcuffs on both his wrists and ankles. Brianna clipped the chain to each set of cuffs, cinching it tightly so that he didn't have much movement. The ghost smiled up at the witch as she helped him roll on his back and said, "I love you and enjoy your little chat with this *child*."

The ghost ethereally slipped out of Jess's body, looking tired but invigorated at the same time. He left the bedroom as Brianna got up and grabbed the blood caked belt off the floor. She glared at her boyfriend as she climbed back on the bed.

She smacked Jess on his face several times as she coldly growled, "Wake up, Jess. Wake up, we need to talk."

He jerked awake, feeling confused and disorientated. Jess focused his bleary gaze on Brianna and said, "Bri? What's going on?" He felt the cold metal of the handcuffs digging into his back. Jess struggled to free himself but to no avail. He glared at her and demanded, "What's the meaning of this? Untie me *now*!"

"Like you don't remember what you did to me earlier," Brianna scoffed incredulously.

"I didn't do anything to you, Bri!" Jess retorted, his anger growing as he shook his body, "You know damn well that I don't like being tied up!"

"After how you abused me earlier, I felt like this would be an effective way to get through to you," Brianna stated as tears welled up in her eyes, but she refused to let them flow.

"You're fucking crazy, Brianna! I didn't hurt you! Quit being a drama queen and let me go!"

The witch cocked an eyebrow as she sat up on her knees and turned her back to him, revealing the damage to her ass, "Care to explain this? *You* did this to me, you bastard!"

Jess's eyes widened, "You think that I did that? I never touched you!"

"So, you say, yet here's your belt that you beat me with," Brianna retorted as she turned to face him, shaking his belt in his face.

Jess's face contorted in disgust, dismissively stating, "How could I? I've been passed out in here this whole time. I'm confident that *you* did that to yourself. You would blame me for it."

"And how did I manage that? You bound my wrists and beat me," the witch replied, showing the bruising on her wrists, glaring at her boyfriend.

"My mother was right about you. You're nothing but an attention seeking, mentally challenged bitch that chooses not to work."

"Are you sure that she wasn't talking about you?" Brianna said as she crawled off the bed, tossing the belt on the floor. She hobbled out of the bedroom, causing Jess to cry out, "Where the hell are you going?"

"I'm going to work on a few website orders. You can join me, if you wish. I won't stop you."

"Release me, Bri!" Jess shouted, panic laced his voice as she shut the bedroom door, "Don't leave me like this! I seriously don't remember hurting you!"

The witch leaned against the door, wondering if he was being honest about it. She knew that he could be a jerk and took pleasure in verbally bashing her, but this was the first time that he got physical with her. She pressed her forehead against the door, her hands pressed on it as she asked, "What is the last thing that you remember?"

"You mean before waking up to your crazy ass?" Jess snapped. When Brianna didn't speak, he got worried that she might leave him like this so he thought about it. His voice softened as he added, "I was playing Wow, doing a dungeon run and-"

"And what else?" Brianna prodded, curious at what he would say next.

Jess thought hard, sweat glistening on his forehead. He grimaced as he bit out, "Nothing. Okay, Bri. I don't get it. I wasn't *that* drunk...was I?"

The witch looked over at his desk and saw the six pack of beer and noticed that two were open. She bit the inside of her cheek, knowing that it would normally take more than that to render him unconscious. She heard panic in his voice once again, "Please let me go, Bri. I'm freaking late for work. I need to call my manager!"

The witch nodded to herself as she walked over to his desk and grabbed his phone. She hobbled back into the bedroom and gingerly sat down on the bed next to him. She unlocked his phone and showed him the call log and said, "You called in sick several hours ago. See? Do you not remember that?"

Jess's face paled, fear crossing over his face as he bit out, his voice shaky, "No, I don't. Brianna? What's happening to me?"

"I'm not sure, but we'll figure this out," Brianna said sympathetically, but then she got close to his face and added with a hint of malice, "Just know that if you touch me like you did tonight, I'll bind you again and drag you down to the creek and let you float out of my life for good. Got it, Jess?"

Jess's mouth gaped open in shock, but he shook his head emphatically, "Yes, dear. Now will you please let me go? I gotta pee."

The witch sighed as she reached for the key. She rolled Jess on his belly and unlocked the cuffs and unclipped the chain. Jess rubbed his wrists as he slowly got out of bed, shuffling towards the bathroom, he said, "I'm so stiff, especially my knees. How long was I bound?"

"Not long," Brianna replied, stifling a chuckle, "but you did do a lot of exertion before then."

The witch wondered if Jess was being influenced in some way by the shadowy thing. If this is true, then Brianna had a feeling that she needed to deal with this dark entity and soon.

Chapter Fourteen

A week had passed since Jess was possessed by Daniel. He was still feeling confused by the whole ordeal, but Brianna never spoke of it. She didn't want to let him know about her little possession tryst with the ghost. The witch wasn't sure if Daniel's tormentor was actually behind Jess's behavior, but as the days went on, her intuition strongly swayed her to the idea.

Jess stepped out of the shower, drying off as Brianna set the table for dinner. He saw two tan ceramic dishes and two glasses of milk and he groaned slightly, "Let me guess, tomato sauce noodles?"

"Yes," the witch replied, knowing that he was going to whine about it, "I'm not feeling up to cooking and this is quick and easy on me to make."

Jess sat down as she put a medium pot down on a hot pad, "You could have just tossed a frozen pizza in the oven. That doesn't take any effort."

"True," Brianna replied as she sat down, spooning the elbow noodles and watery tomato sauce on his dish, "but you wanted to sleep in before going to work so it wouldn't have been done in time. Especially since you decided on taking a shower. Would you prefer a hot pocket?"

"Anything would be better than *this*," Jess scowled as he grabbed his spoon and ate it.

"*Momma?*" The conure sweetly said as he eyed Brianna, "*Yum yum, please? Midnight loves momma!*"

The witch rolled her eyes as she portioned out seven noodles on her bowl. She walked slowly over to Midnight's cage and put the pasta into his food dish. The conure bobbed his head and said, "*Thank you! Good momma!*"

Brianna sat back down and spooned more tomato sauce noodles into her dish. Jess glanced up at her and asked, "Have you heard back from any of those companies yet?"

Brianna added salt and pepper to her meal, "Nothing yet. Just the usual no-reply emails confirming that they received it."

Jess glanced at his watch, debating if he should go in to work or not. The witch admonished, "If and when I do get an offer, you have to go to work. You know as well as I do that we can't survive on my income alone."

Jess dramatically sighed as spooned more noodles into his mouth, "I wish that they would hurry up and call you. This job is wearing me down. I need a day shift, not these boring nights."

"I understand," Brianna said as she sat her spoon down and looked him square in his eyes, "but you need to keep this job. I'm not sure if I'll even get a call and I don't want to go living in motels again. My health can't take it."

Jess huffed as he finished his dinner and downed his milk. He wiped his mouth and said, "Fine. Fine, I'll go in. At least see if you can find some numbers and call those companies. Try to be more proactive. It might get them to notice you."

"I'll see what I can find," the witch replied as she sipped her milk. Jess stood up, walked over and kissed her on the cheek. He looked out the window and saw that it was raining hard. Jess grabbed his hooded jacket and walked over to the front door. As he opened it, Jess grumbled under his breath and ran straight to the car, leaving the door wide open.

The headlights from the car shined brightly in the cabin, the rain came down hard, looking like a waterfall. The witch stood up, scowling as she walked over to the front door to close it. As Jess backed up and drove away, a shadowy figure stood on the porch.

Brianna couldn't see anything that resembled any facial features, yet she could tell that it was menacingly glaring at her. Its malicious hate sent an uneasy sense of dread in the witch's body as it spoke, *"Did you enjoy the thrashing from your boyfriend? It will pale in comparison to what I-"*

"Oh, shut your mouth and leave *our* home. You're not welcome here." Brianna interrupted the shadowy thing's tirade, her face devoid of all emotions except contempt.

The dark entity chuckled, *"Brave talk from the bitchy little witch. Step outside and get rid of me, if you dare."*

"If you're so powerful, come in here and deal with me," the witch challenged with a smirk, "Oh, that's right. I'd have to allow you to enter because you're too much of a pussy to pass through my simple protections. That's gotta sting that over-inflated dark ego of yours a bit, huh?"

The shadowy thing roared as it rushed at the witch. It bounced off the unseen barrier like a tennis ball, further infuriating it. The dark entity clawed and attacked the protective barrier, but couldn't get to his target. Brianna felt each blow to her shielding since she was connected to it, but she stood her ground.

The shadowy thing hissed as it slowly backed away, pointing a tendril at her, *"I will find a way in here and then I'll add you and Jess to my collection."*

"Don't spend all night thinking about how you'll do, it makes wrinkles and will ruin your dark complexion. I hope you're not too tired. The wolves are coming," the witch mocked as she slammed the door shut. The dark entity glared at the cabin door and vanished as the wolves approached.

Brianna marched towards the bedroom, determined to put an end to this malevolent entity. Silverwolf and several of the spirit wolves entered the cabin, following close behind her.

"Are you going to do something about that thing tonight," Silver snarled, itching for a fight.

As she grabbed her ritual supplies, Daniel appeared with fear and worry on his ethereal visage, "*It's too powerful. You could get killed, just like me and my family were all those years ago.*"

"I'm not going to live in fear in my new home," Brianna replied as she grabbed the box with her supplies and struggled to walk out with it.

"*I don't want to lose you, my sweet little Bri. That thing has taken so much from me already.*"

"She won't be alone, *ghost*," Silver growled, "If you're so scared, you can go hide in the woods!"

"*I'm scared for her. I already know what it's capable of doing. It will find a way in here.*"

As the witch set the box on the floor, she smiled as she walked over and grabbed the salt container, "Do tell everything that you have witnessed it doing. As Silver said, I won't be alone in this fight, but we need to create a plan of attack. I want you by my side when we do this, so go outside to the creek and gather more power. Have faith in me. We *will* end him tonight, my love."

Daniel nodded and solemnly replied before leaving, "*I do, just be ready for anything. The shadowy thing is a cunning and tricky creature.*"

Chapter Fifteen

Jess glared out of the windshield as the wipers barely kept up with the deluge of rainfall. He sped along the wet highway, darting in and out of traffic. He was irritated that he had no choice but to go to work, especially in this weather.

"I'm going to be soaking wet all night," Jess bitterly spat out as he reached into the fast-food bag for a few fries that he picked up along the way. He hated it when Brianna made her poor man's pasta so he decided that if he was going to be miserable at work, why not enjoy his favorite food there?

Jess shoveled the fries into his mouth like he hadn't eaten in a week, his fingers covered in salt and grease. He grumbled as he turned down his exit, "What I wouldn't give to be the one at home. Brianna could be a little more grateful."

An eerie voice coldly remarked next to his ear, causing the hairs on the back of Jess's neck to stand up, *"Pull over and I can grant that wish for you, Jess."*

He panicked as swerved by several cars, making his way recklessly into the parking lot of a shopping mall as a number of horns blared at him. Jess hit the brakes, causing the car to skid to an abrupt halt. He put the car in park and nervously looked all around him, fearing to actually look in the backseat.

"Who's there!" Jess nervously bit out, his heart racing faster than the rain pounding on his car.

No response.

Jess leaned forward with his hands on the sides of his head, resting his sweaty forehead on the steering wheel, "I must be cracking up. That's the only explanation!"

A chuckle from the backseat caused him to freeze with his eyes bulging, "*My dear boy. There's always another explanation for the things that you don't understand. I just so happen to be one of those.*"

Jess's body quaked, fearing that whomever it was in the car meant him harm. He felt paralyzed, all thoughts of fleeing his car seemed impossible.

"What," Jess gulped hard, not daring to look at the rearview mirror, "What do you want with me? I-I have no money-"

"*It's not what I want from you, Jess,*" the shadowy thing said calmly, trying to soothe him, "*I have a little proposal for you, if you're willing to listen to what I have to say.*"

"I'm not-" Jess stammered, "sex is not what you're asking for, is it?"

"*What I want is what you have. All that I ask from you is to turn the vehicle around and go home,*" the dark entity spoke as it slipped several of its ethereal tendrils into Jess's body. He grimaced in pain as the shadowy thing added, "*I can give you the life that you truly desire. All you have to do is go back to the cabin and you'll never have to worry about money ever again. I can make it happen, if you do as I ask.*"

"What's your name?"

The shadowy thing laughed, "*My name is inconsequential. It's too long and you lack the ability to say it properly. Just know that I'm in the wish granting business.*"

"So, you're like what? A genie?"

"If it helps your confused mind to call me that, then yes, I am," the shadowy thing replied, rolling its non-existent eyes, barely containing a sigh, *"Now tell me Jess, what do you truly desire?"*

"I want enough money so I can get a place for myself. Something better than that damn cabin. Enough wealth so I don't have to even need to work again," Jess replied as he finally glanced at the rearview mirror, seeing the dark entity for the first time, "Can you truly do this for me?"

"And what about the girl?"

Jess snorted, "Brianna can stay in that shit hole for all I care. I'm tired of her holding me back from my true potential. She doesn't respect me. Never has and never will. If I'm well off, she can manage on her own. I don't owe Brianna Monk a *damn* thing!"

"Hmm, it sounds as if you're not that fond of her anymore. For this wish to be granted, a payment must be made. Magic like this always comes with a price, my dear boy," the shadowy thing said as it slithered more tendrils into Jess.

"And-" Jess painfully grunted, "and what is the price?"

The dark entity whispered into his ear and said, *"Head back to the cabin and I'll gladly name it. Do it, Jess! Your fortune is waiting for you, if you're willing to listen to me."*

Jess smiled greedily as he shifted the car into gear and made his way back to the highway, to return to the cabin.

Chapter Sixteen

"What do you mean Jess hasn't shown up?" Brianna spoke on the phone with his manager. "He left for work an hour ago."

"I've been trying to call and text Jess, but I haven't heard back from him. Hopefully, he's okay. It's flooding in areas around town," Steve stated with a hint of both worry and irritation in his voice.

"If I can get a hold of him, I'll let you know. Is this a good number to call you on?"

"Yes. This is my work cell. If he shows up, I will call you back so you don't have to worry so much."

"A text will suffice," Brianna replied, "I have a lot of health issues and it's difficult talking on the phone. I have a hard time tracking the conversations."

"Say no more, Brianna" Steve sincerely replied, *"I can relate to what you're saying. I have a child in a similar situation. I'll text you if and when Jess shows up. Take care."*

"You too," the witch said as the call ended. She sent Jess several texts, asking if he was okay and mentioning that his supervisor was asking about him.

No response.

She sat her phone down on the counter, concern nagging at her mind. Brianna wasn't sure if Jess got caught in the storm somewhere or simply decided to blow off going to work entirely. Daniel looked at her as he placed a hand on her shoulder, "*I know that you're worried about him. Are you sure that you want to deal with the shadowy thing tonight?*"

"I can't wait any longer. I *must* rid my home of this entity if either of us are going to have any peace." Brianna said as she made a smaller circle with black salt to contain the shadowy thing and charged it with her magic.

One of the spirit wolves ran into the cabin, going directly to Silverwolf. The alpha suspiciously squinted his eyes as he ordered, "Keep your distance and report back here immediately."

"What's going on, Silver," the witch asked as she sat down in the middle of the salt circle, lighting incense with the flame of a black candle.

"Jess's car is heading this way. From what I've been told, he's not alone," Silver replied as he looked at her, "You ready for this?"

"I have no choice, but I know that this ends tonight," Brianna replied as she grabbed her athame and held it against her body. "Everyone knows what to do. Be ready to strike."

Daniel nodded as he slipped out of the cabin, along with the other entities that the witch had called upon to help her in this supernatural fight. The unmistakable squealing of brakes let the witch know that Jess had returned. She wondered if he couldn't make it to work and decided to come home instead. The fact that something else was in the car with him didn't sit well with her because no one said that this other person was a human.

As the witch closed and fully charged her own circle, the cabin door was forcefully swung open. Jess stood at the threshold, soaking wet and breathing hard as he glared at the witch with contempt, "Hello, Bri. Did you miss me?"

"Bad boy! Not daddy!" Midnight screamed. He puffed up and yanked violently at the latch on his cage, but couldn't get it opened because of the clip lock.

Brianna could sense a change in Jess. His posture was different than usual and his body looked bulkier, like he had grown massive. His eyes were as black as obsidian that held an unspoken promise of pain and suffering. Both of his fists were clenched, like he was ready to fight. Jess groaned as he stepped in the cabin, causing the witch's protections to warn her of an otherworldly intruder.

"Shouldn't you be at work? Why are you back here?" the witch asked, knowing full well that this wasn't her boyfriend.

"I chose to return home and add you to my collection," Jess replied, his voice sounding more like the dark entity. Brianna feigned shock and surprise as he added, "I told you that I'd find a way in here to get you, little witch."

"Take your hold off of him, this fight is between you and me."

"Jess is not here. I've collected him already," the shadowy thing said as it slowly stalked towards the witch, "He was easy enough to dupe. I promised him financial gains in exchange for bringing me into the cabin. The fool offered you up willingly and I, being a generous being, accepted it. Though, the price for this little ruse was paid as soon as we arrived."

Brianna felt the stings from each word it said, like the belt beating she had endured a week ago. Jess willingly left her out as an offering to the shadowy thing, but ended up paying the ultimate price, "You killed him?"

"Yes, and you're next you pathetic excuse of a witch. I'll-" the dark entity's mocking was interrupted as Daniel flew into Jess's body, dislodging it from the dead body. Jess's body crumbled down on the floor as the shadowy thing hovered next to it, "*Your torture will be slow and painful, Daniel! I'll deal with-*"

At once, the shadowy thing was swarmed by a huge number of the four different elementals. The spirit wolves latched their teeth into the dark entity, dragging it into the small black salt circle, containing it so that it couldn't escape.

The shadowy thing snarled and yelled at Brianna, "*You filthy bitch! You're not much of a witch if you have to rely on these things to do your bidding! I'll be free soon enough and then I'll kill all of you!*"

Confusion assailed the dark entity as his captors all laughed at it. The shadowy thing bellowed, "*What's so damn funny, witch?*"

"You are. You keep assuming that I'm just a little witch. I am one, but," Brianna stood up, her hair floating all around her as Gaia appeared behind her with a smirk, "I'm also a Warrior of Gaia and it's time to pay for *all* of your transgressions!"

The shadowy thing's darkness paled significantly, it's ethereal form quivered, "*No! You can't be! It's not possible! Be merciful, Brianna!*"

The witch smirked as she pointed her athame at the cowering entity as Daniel watched on in awe, "All the lives you hurt. All the souls that you tortured leaves no room for mercy!" She glanced at the ghost for a split second and then continued, "Sending you back into the abyss is not nearly enough of a punishment for you! My allies and I are going to shed you until you no longer exist."

"Yeah! Get him momma! Ow bad boy!" Midnight chirped as he added his own magic to the fight.

Brianna focused her own magic through her athame as she slashed it at the shadowy thing, carving it to pieces as the wolves tore more chunks from it. The dark entity cried out in pain, still pleading for mercy, but it fell on deaf ears. The elementals kept their tight hold on the shadowy thing until there was nothing left.

The witch dropped down to the floor, feeling the effects of her magic and the exertion. She felt a hand on each of her shoulders, one was cold and the other warm. Brianna smiled at Daniel as he had a blissful glow across his visage. She placed her hand on top of his and said as tears trickled down her face, "Your dark captor is no more. Go, be with your family. I'm sure that they miss you."

"*But,*" the ghost stammered slightly, "*what about you, my sweet little Bri? Do you want me to leave you?*"

"You can do what you want, Daniel," Gaia said in a stern, but caring voice, "If you want to be reunited with your family, that is your choice, but I would advise against it."

"What do you mean by that, Gaia," the witch turned her attention to her patron goddess. The goddess glanced at her warrior for a moment, focused her gaze on the ghost. Daniel felt like he was in trouble and wasn't sure he was going to like Her reply

"Your family was absorbed by that creature. If you move on, they won't be there waiting for you. I believe you have suffered enough at the hands of your dark murderer; it wouldn't be right to allow your suffering to continue. So, I say again, what do you choose, Daniel Powell?"

The ghost's shoulders slouched as he moved away from the others, his sadness evident. As Daniel thought about what Gaia just said, Brianna released the magic from both circles and gave thanks to all who helped her. The witch was eager to go to the ghost and comfort him. She slid a finger through the salt circle and was about to stand up and go over to him, but was held in place by the goddess.

She looked up at the deity, her eyes pleading as said, "Please, Gaia. Let me go to him. Daniel needs me now more than ever."

"I know this is how you feel," Gaia replied, not revealing her emotions to her warrior, "but Daniel is going to have to make a choice. I don't want you to sway him. His answer will dictate what comes next in his journey."

The ghost slowly made his way to the goddess, his head cast down. His eyes were focused solely on the witch, and seeing her like this made him sadly smile, "*My greatest fears have come to pass. The shadowy thing made sure that I'd never be reunited with my family. I've been a lost soul for so long that I never thought I'd know happiness or love ever again, until I met you, Brianna. If I have to choose, I'd choose an eternity of suffering if I can't be with you. I love you, Brianna Monk! I chose you, my sweet little Bri! I choose to haunt you for the rest of our existence."*

"Oh, Daniel," Brianna's lips parted and slightly quivering, "Are you sure you want to be with me?"

"I confess my love and devotion before everyone here, as witnesses to my decision to my lover. Is that okay, um, Gaia?"

"No," the deity replied as she moved away from Brianna. She turned her head to look at the ghost and added, "You'll *not* be haunting my warrior. That's not good enough for either of you. Will you be truly devoted to her? Can you treat Brianna better than Jess?"

"In a fucking heartbeat!" Daniel snapped at the goddess. His eyes widened as he cupped his hands over his mouth. Gaia cocked her head to the side, looking amused by the ghost's outburst. He moved next to the goddess and said, *"Excuse the harshness of my answer. I've seen how that boy treated her. It disgusted me to no end. I know that I can and will be the partner that she deserves! I vow it to you!"*

Gaia placed her hands on the ghost's shoulders and briefly smiled. Her visage became serious as she addressed her warrior, "Brianna! Do *you* accept his choice?"

The witch stood up and stepped out of the salt circle and stood next to Daniel, not taking her eyes off the goddess, "I do, but why does it matter what I think? He made the choice to stay by my side and I couldn't be any happier."

"Because it involves you as well. You've had to endure many hardships throughout your life. You need this as much as he does. Do you accept Daniel?" Gaia replied, her eyes glowing fiercely.

"I do, Gaia," she replied with a hint of remorse, "I wish that I could hold him. I know that's me just being selfish-"

"*I want that as well, my sweet little Bri. I couldn't ask for a better woman to love,*" Daniel said as she brushed the back of his hand against her wet cheek, causing her to shiver. At that moment, another entity appeared next to Gaia. Brianna wasn't exactly sure who this being was, but could tell that it was another deity.

The witch could see that He was Native American with long flowing black hair that had been braided. He wore no shirt, but had a tattoo of a bear paw and a wolf paw intertwined to look like a heart on his chest. The god didn't bother wearing any clothes and seemed to not care, like a free spirit, as he grinned.

"Are you willing to do this, EnergyBear?" Gaia asked. She glanced at him and added, "If yes, then I'll pay you with favor."

The god inspected the room, noting the dead body and the salt circles, still grinning, "Looks like someone had a party and didn't invite me. Am I here to provide cleaning services?"

Gaia rolled her eyes and said with a huff, "You know *exactly* why I called for you. Will you do it?"

"You know that I can't resist helping you. I've been watching and listening, ever since you told me about this situation," EnergyBear said as he squatted down by Jess's lifeless form. He placed a hand on the cold corpse and added, "Don't fret. I kept him prepped as soon as he dropped."

"What's going on, Bri?" Daniel looked nervous, *"What are they up to?"*

"I'm not sure, my love, but I think that we're about to find out," the witch replied as the god looked at her and the ghost.

He smiled and Brianna could feel so much positive energy and power flooding the cabin that she couldn't help but feel love and comfort. EnergyBear said to Gaia, "Payment is not necessary. I'll gladly do this for free. The love that I see in these two is payment enough. Besides, MoonRose would tan my hide if I refused this small task. Though I'd enjoy it, she's great at handing out punishment!"

"Very well," the goddess said as she motioned with her hand, "Brianna. Daniel. Step forward and let EnergyBear do this for you both."

They both did as Gaia asked, but as they stood next to Jess, the witch asked the god, "What are you going to do? Will it hurt us?"

EnergyBear placed a hand on his heart, making a pouting face, "Oh, I'm wounded by your ignorance. I suppose that Gaia hasn't told you about me and my role in all of this?" When Brianna shook her head, he continued on, "I'm a Native American god of creation, master of life, death, and resurrection. I'm here to bring your boyfriend back to life. Isn't that wonderful?"

"Then why do you need me?" Daniel spat out, feeling confused, *"Why are you bringing this boy back to life?"*

"But *you're* the boyfriend I'm referring to, you silly little spirit." EnergyBear said as he pointed at Brianna, "Did you really think that she wanted that abusive turd back? I've taken the liberty of taking Jess's soul and I'll be handing it over to MoonRose for punishment. That's why I'm not taking payment from Gaia, despite it being quite the generous offer."

"Oh," the ghost sheepishly replied, *"Will this hurt?"*

"Yes. This is not your original body so there *will* be a lot of pain and suffering, but it will pass as you acclimate to your new vessel," the god looked at the witch and reassuringly added, "Don't fret, little one. This is to be expected and I'll be dropping in daily to ease his suffering. One must endure pain in order to properly heal. Do I have your permission to come in and heal him?"

"Why? Didn't you just pop in here without it?" Brianna asked.

"Special circumstances. When you called for aid in your battle, I took it as an open invitation. It's bad form to enter without being invited, though I can if need be. I'll even heal you while I'm here, if you want."

"Daniel will need it more than I will," the witch shrugged her shoulders, "You have my permission to come and go as you please, but do behave while you're here, or I'll revoke it."

EnergyBear grinned at Gaia, "You taught this one well," the god reached out and grabbed Daniel, guiding him into Jess's body. He also took the witch by her hand and said,

"Sit down, deary. This will take a while, so you might as well get comfortable."

EnergyBear chanted and sang a Native American song, causing Brianna to lie down and fall fast asleep as the god's energy coursed throughout her little body.

Chapter Seventeen
Three months later

Brianna sat at her desk, toiling away at another website build. Several weeks after the battle with the shadowy thing, she received a call from a company called MoonRose Creations. They were happy with her portfolio that she submitted and were more than willing to work with her, giving her a flexible schedule because of her disability, as long as she could fill the backorders.

Anytime Brianna completed her assignments in a timely fashion, the company gave her a bonus check on top of her regular salary, which was often. The company gave her a generous benefits package despite being an independent contractor because they didn't want to lose her productivity. She signed the contract with one stipulation: if her health deteriorated and she had to take time off to recover, the time would be covered, no questions asked, citing the ADA for reasonable accommodations.

Brianna was still considered disabled by her doctor, but she got the green light to work since she could set her own schedule and hours. The witch smiled lovingly as a pair of muscular arms wrapped around her chest, the scent of soil and cedar assailed her nostrils.

"How's this build coming along, my sweet little Bri?" Daniel asked as he kissed the top of her head.

"Just a few last-minute tweaks and it will be done. How's dinner coming along?"

"The pot roast is pretty much done. I added the potatoes and carrots a little while ago, so it should be ready in a few more minutes. The bread is cooling on the counter and the table is set, my love."

Daniel now worked with an agricultural company, using the computer knowledge that Jess had and combined it with his old-world farming ingenuity. He managed to find the perfect niche as he learned more about modern society. Daniel worked on repairing both the farming equipment and any computer glitches.

The foreman was astounded and amazed at Daniel's skills. He never saw someone as gifted with the machines and knowing what the land required for a great yield of crops. *It's like he had a six sense for what everything needed,* his boss proudly commented.

At that moment, there was a knock on the door. Brianna looked up at Daniel and said, "Time to pretend, *Jess.*"

Daniel nodded as he stood up. The witch could see that he looked like Jess, but as the days passed, he looked more like himself as he did when he was a specter. Daniel had trimmed down; his muscles had more definition that could only come from manual labor. He walked over and opened the front door and was greeted by Anna and Lee with William and Jane bringing up the rear.

"Come on in! Dinner is almost ready," Daniel jovially announced as he motioned for them to come inside.

"Jess," Lee said as he shook his hand, "you're looking well."

"Life's been good to me as of late," Daniel smirked as he glanced at Brianna's mother,

"Did you both have a pleasant drive over here?"

"It would have been had *someone* stopped a bit more," Anna glared at her husband as she walked over to her daughter and hugged her, "How are you doing, my dear?"

"I'm managing. It's good to see you again, mom," Brianna smiled lovingly at her.

Anna glanced down at the computer screen, "I know that you're busy these days, but can you spare a minute away from work?"

The witch turned and reached for the mouse. She clicked the save button and wrote a little note to herself and said, "I can now, mom. Just needed to write a reminder of where to pick up again. Let's go sit at the table."

They made their way to the kitchen table as William and Jane came through the door. She hugged her son and said, "Jess, are you doing alright. You look different."

"A brush with death can have that effect on a person," Daniel replied as he looked at Brianna with a warm smile. The couple used the cover story that he nearly died on his way to work and had some brain trauma as a result. "I wouldn't be here without her help."

"You lost a lot of weight, my boy," William smiled lovingly at Daniel, while Jane glared at the witch as she waddled into the cabin.

"It's from working in the field and a better diet," Daniel replied as he walked with his father to the dining room table.

"Is the food ready? I'm starving," Jane blurted out.

"Almost, *mother*," Daniel bristled, trying to remain calm, "I'm sure that you would rather eat a fully cooked meal rather than raw vegetables?"

"Hmph," Jess's mother said bitterly as she scowled at Brianna, "It should have been ready as soon as we got here. Why can't you do anything right? If you can't cook a decent dinner, then why bother?"

"Because she's not the one that cooking it," Daniel slammed his fist on the table, causing everyone to jump. His anger towards the woman was obvious. Brianna rubbed his thigh, trying to calm him down, but he continued as he pointed a finger at the front door, "Just for once in your miserable, ungrateful life, leave my sweet little Bri alone. If you can't wait a couple of minutes, there's the door!"

Everyone at the table sat in silence, shocked by Daniel's outburst. The witch glanced around at the others, gauging their reactions. Anna had the slightest smirk, looking impressed. Lee's mouth gaped open. William had concern etched into his usual laid-back visage. Jane looked both speechless and indignant, turning a deep shade of red with anger.

"How dare you speak to your mother like that!" Jane bit out, "I don't know what *she* has done to you, but you need to show me some respect!"

Daniel menacingly eyed her and coldly replied, "Respect goes both ways. If you can't be civil in *our* home, then you're not welcome here."

He stood up and sliced the loaf of bread and placed it on the table. Anna looked at Brianna and said, "Jess, you should sit down and let us serve dinner."

Daniel turned around with the crockpot in his hands and emphatically stated, "No, ma'am. Brianna has been working hard all day. You and Lee just drove over eight hours to get here. It's the least that I can do. I'd say that my *mother* should do it, but I'm sure that we will all starve waiting on her."

Jane was about to argue, but Daniel locked his eyes with hers, his eyes were glowing white, "I insist and I won't take any more arguments in this matter, *mother*."

Jane looked down at her place and he ladled the pot roast on her plate and placed a slice of bread on the side of her place. Daniel served everyone and sat several different sodas on the table. The witch grabbed his hand as he sat down and said, "Thanks, *Jess*. I love you!"

"And I love you too, my sweet little Bri," Daniel replied as he leaned down and kissed her on her lips. Everyone ate in peace with no more arguing.

About the Author

Joshua Griffith is a Native American Cherokee who loves to tell stories about the paranormal and the supernatural, but adds a twist of humor to alleviate some of the inherent drama and suspense that can make the characters seem more relatable. He grew up in eastern part of Oklahoma, witnessing many strange and wondrous things that went bump in the night. Joshua Griffith currently resides in the Pacific Northwest. As part of his path as an energy healer, Joshua Griffith felt it would be good idea to incorporate some of his experiences in his novels. As they say, there's always a hint of truth even in a good work of fiction so it's up to you to decide which is truth and which is hot air. Joshua Griffith invites you to read his stories with an open mind because these tales are works of fiction, but ask yourself this: Could this really happen?

If you enjoyed A Ghostly Affair, please do leave a review. I love reading them because they encourage me to get better and keep the stories coming!

www.ingramcontent.com/pod-product-compliance
Lightning Source LLC
Chambersburg PA
CBHW060545260626
47161CB00003B/1066